COMMON SENSE

COMMON SENSE

COLIN WREFORD

Copyright © 2022 Colin Wreford

The moral right of the author has been asserted.

Apart from any fair dealing for the purposes of research or private study, or criticism or review, as permitted under the Copyright, Designs and Patents Act 1988, this publication may only be reproduced, stored or transmitted, in any form or by any means, with the prior permission in writing of the publishers, or in the case of reprographic reproduction in accordance with the terms of licences issued by the Copyright Licensing Agency. Enquiries concerning reproduction outside those terms should be sent to the publishers.

This is a work of fiction. Names, characters, businesses, places, events and incidents are either the products of the author's imagination or used in a fictitious manner. Any resemblance to actual persons, living or dead, or actual events is purely coincidental.

Matador
Unit E2 Airfield Business Park,
Harrison Road, Market Harborough,
Leicestershire. LE16 7WB
Tel: 0116 2792299
Email: books@troubador.co.uk
Web: www.troubador.co.uk/matador
Twitter: @matadorbooks

ISBN 978 1803130 408

British Library Cataloguing in Publication Data.
A catalogue record for this book is available from the British Library.

Printed and bound in Great Britain by 4edge Limited
Typeset in 12pt Minion Pro by Troubador Publishing Ltd, Leicester, UK

Matador is an imprint of Troubador Publishing Ltd

I dedicate this book to my late parents – Jack and Betty – for their life-long love and support. I am sure they are watching me proudly from above.

CHAPTER 1

2029 GENERAL ELECTION

May 2029

"Hello, my name is Sara Molan, and welcome to the morning show dedicated to yesterday's general election here in the UK. For those of you who have not been with us all night, I will start by announcing the results so far. There are two Northern Ireland seats that have not yet declared, but I can announce that the UK has a new prime minister and a brand new party in control of the House of Commons. Yes, the Common Sense Party has broken the mould of British politics with a resounding victory, claiming 400 seats. This leaves the Conservatives and the Labour Party with ninety-nine seats each. Common Sense will have an overall majority in the House of Commons. Shortly, I hope to be talking to my revered broadcasting colleague, David McDougall, the joint leader of the new ruling party and, presumably, our next prime minister.

In the meantime, I will hand you over to my regional colleagues to discuss the results where you live."

Once off air for a few minutes, Sara seeks clarification from her floor manager about the next segment of the programme.

"Well, the good news is that the new prime minister is in the building, so you can interview him as soon as we go back on air," says the floor manager. "The bad news is that you are going to have to think on your feet."

Sara looks puzzled. "I've worked with David for years. He's not going to faze me just because he's the prime minister."

"That's the problem. Bob Godwin has come in saying he's taking charge of Common Sense, and I don't know what you know about him, but the rest of us know sod all."

As the floor manager finishes speaking, a group of people enter the studio. In the middle of the group, almost hidden by bodyguards and armed police, is Bob Godwin.

"Two minutes to air time," is the message in Sara's earphones as she returns to her chair.

The floor manager eases Bob Godwin into the other seat at the news desk.

"Why are you here and not David?" Sara asks Mr Godwin as her earphones give her the message that she is on air in one minute.

"Because I am now the sole leader of the Common Sense Party and have been asked to form the next government," he replies.

"Right, well, we're on air in twenty seconds, so we'll just have to wing it," Sara confirms to her guest, and then she immediately addresses the viewers. "Welcome back to the morning programme looking at the results of yesterday's general election. I have a very special guest with me this morning: the new Prime Minster of the UK, Mr Robert Godwin." Turning to her guest, Sara continues seamlessly, "Mr Godwin, welcome to the studio, and congratulations on your party's resounding success. My first question – as many of our audience would be expecting to see my colleague David McDougall in that chair – is could you explain who is taking charge of the party and the country?"

"Hello Sara and hello to all the viewers. Yes, I would like to thank everyone who has placed their votes and faith in the Common Sense Party. I can assure you that everyone in the party will do everything possible to deliver our manifesto promises and sort out the many problems facing this great country. David and I have been joint leaders since the party was formed just three years ago. He has done a superb job in fronting our general election campaign, but obviously, there can only be one prime minister, and I am delighted to say that the executive committee has decided overnight that I should now have the honour of leading the party on my own. I have been to Buckingham Palace earlier today and have been invited by King Charles the Third to form the next government."

"Perhaps, then, you could tell the viewers something about yourself?"

"Well, I was born in Plymouth, Devon, and am an only child. I left school at sixteen and started work selling second-hand cars for someone else before setting up my own car-sales business in Plymouth. I sold that three years ago, and I have concentrated on politics ever since. I am fifty-one years old and divorced, with no children that I am aware of. I am simply delighted to have the chance to turn our many brilliant policies into legislation and create a better life for us all."

"With all due respect, Mr Godwin, running this country is rather more challenging than running a car-sales business."

"Sara, I strongly disagree with you. The basic principles are the same. There is the need to balance the books and keep the customers happy. At the moment, the economy is still struggling from the eight-year-long Covid-19 pandemic, but I believe we have the policies to get things back on an even keel. Our manifesto states no tax rises, and I am delighted to have the opportunity here and now to confirm that I will honour that promise, along with all the other promises we have made during the campaign."

"Your manifesto is rather short on details, so perhaps you could tell us your priorities and how you will achieve your aims?"

"The number one priority is to reduce crime, which is running at appalling levels. I have a clear mandate from the electorate to achieve this, and I make a promise today that crime will be reduced by at least 80% by the end of this Parliament. I can confirm a few measures today, but full details will be in the justice bill, which will be put before Parliament as soon as possible. As promised in our manifesto, capital punishment will be reintroduced for all murderers. Corporal punishment will be used in schools and the judicial system. All prison sentences will be served in full, and I shall be building ten new prisons plus twenty new regional punishment centres in the next twelve months. This will provide short- and long-term employment for the construction industry, as well as the prison service. I will also immediately start the process to abolish the unelected House of Lords."

"Prime Minister, some of those ideas are going to attract massive opposition from pro-life and humanitarian groups, as well as within the House of Lords."

"Sara, please call me Bob. Frankly, I couldn't care less what namby-pamby liberals have to say. The British people have clearly stated with their votes that they want a tough approach to crime, and that is exactly what they are going to get. Regarding the House of Lords, our manifesto specifically states that we will be operating a one-chamber system, and I will be abolishing the upper house as a matter of urgency."

"What about the economy? Where is the money coming from to build all these new prisons?"

"I am very aware that the ordinary people in this country have faced hard times for far too long. I cannot promise immediate improvement, but I will get things back on track. The starting point is to withdraw from Mr Johnson's ridiculous trade deal with the EU. Then we will be free to take advantage of President Harris' incredible trade offer, which my predecessor dismissed without a moment's thought. That is the way forward and remember – no tax rises."

"May I go back to the start of our conversation and talk briefly about David McDougall? Will he become deputy prime minister or maybe a Cabinet minister?"

"David has, as I have already said, played a huge part in getting this brand new party elected, and he deserves the highest possible appreciation for his efforts. I am not in a position to tell you who will get which job, as I have to give this matter a lot of thought, but, Sara, you will be amongst the very first to know. I think we need to bring this interview to an end now, as I have a lot of work to do to fulfil every one of the manifesto promises."

"In that case, I hope you will return for another interview when you have completed your choice of ministers."

"Sara, I must say that I will not be doing interviews or holding press conferences. Any information the Government wishes to convey to the media and, more importantly, the electorate will be contained in regular government pronouncements."

On that note, Prime Minister Robert "Bob" Godwin takes off his microphone and exits the studio, surrounded by his entourage.

A slightly flummoxed Sara Molan says hesitatingly to the camera, "Things certainly seem to be changing at the top of British politics. We will go back to our regional stations for a few minutes, and then I will be asking various political figures and commentators for their views on the prime minister's comments. We will be starting with Lord Ashburton and his views on the future of the House of Lords and after that I hope to speak to my good friend David McDougall about what seems to be his rather uncertain political future just hours after being elected. See you all soon."

*

Two days later, Sara Molan is back on air to inform viewers of the fast-moving changes in British politics.

"Hello and welcome to this special programme looking in detail at the latest news from Westminster. Firstly, it has now been confirmed that former prime minister Boris Johnson has resigned as leader of the Conservative Party. In a break from previous leadership changes, the party has announced that Michael Gove will take over as leader of the party with immediate effect. He will, therefore, become joint leader of the opposition with Sir Keir Starmer, the Labour Party leader. To date, the new prime minster, Bob Godwin, has only given one interview, which was with me on the day he took up the position. He has released details today of some of his Cabinet appointments, including

Professor Susan Woodley as deputy prime minister, Simeon Grey as health minister and Neil Harris as chancellor of the exchequer. These, of course, are all new names as none of the Common Sense MPs have ever held any political positions until now. In addition, the prime minister has issued a statement through his official spokesperson saying that his former co-leader, David McDougall, will not be offered a ministerial position. We have asked Mr Godwin to come on this programme to discuss his Cabinet appointments, but his spokesperson has told us that he does not intend to give any interviews at all during his five-year tenure as prime minister. I shall, however, be talking to David McDougall later in the programme. Additionally, today, the Government has issued some details of its justice bill, which will hugely change the judicial systems throughout the UK. I am joined now by Richard Newbury, our political editor. Richard, would you start by taking us through the main changes contained in this bill?" Sara asks.

"Yes, well, this bill has been hyped as the most important change in British justice since the Magna Carta," explains Richard. "I have only seen the headline points as the wording of the actual bill has not yet been released, but it is fair to say that the hype seems to be true for once. Firstly, and possibly most controversially, the jury system is to be abolished, and verdicts will now be decided entirely by a judge or three magistrates, depending on the type of crime being considered.

Secondly, all prison sentences handed down by the courts will now be served in full, and this will also apply to prisoners currently serving their sentences. This is bound to upset human rights and pro-prisoner groups, and it will be interesting to see how the Government reacts to that inevitable opposition. It must be said, though, that many people have been pushing for the early release scheme to be scrapped in recent years. Prison regimes will become much stricter, with the emphasis on discipline and compulsory training. As announced previously, ten new prisons and twenty new punishment centres are to be built. The latter will be required as corporal punishment is to be reintroduced as a sentencing option and as a mandatory legal requirement for some crimes. The bill will also reinstate corporal punishment in schools. Also, parents will now be able to use reasonable physical punishment on their children aged up to eighteen. I understand that the bill itself will contain details of minimum and maximum punishments for all of these different environments."

"Richard, does the bill say anything about capital punishment?"

"It does. We already knew that this was to be introduced for all convicted murderers. The information released today states that executions will be carried out by military firing squads. There are—"

"Sorry, will you just clarify that for me? Is the Government really planning to shoot murderers to death? It just seems incredible."

"Sara, I imagine that the method to be used will come as a shock to a great many people. No details of how the death sentence would be carried out are mentioned in the Common Sense Party's manifesto, so this is the first detailed information published on this matter. It does seem brutal, and I suspect that this will be a major talking point in the coming days. There are, however, other highly controversial policies revealed today. Many crimes will now carry mandatory minimum sentences, and the Government is planning a major assault on our sex lives."

"You must be joking."

"I wish I were joking. Homosexuality will be banned under this bill, as will vaginal sex outside marriage. The age of consent will remain at sixteen, but anyone convicted of having sex with an underage partner will face at least six months' imprisonment. The minimum age of criminal responsibility, which is currently ten years old, is to be completely abolished. If all this isn't enough to keep us awake tonight, the final part of the bill introduces branding as a punishment for all rapists, paedophiles and adulterers. I fear we will have to wait for the actual bill to find out exactly what this involves. We do know persistent sex offenders will be branded as sluts. Clamping down on prostitution will also be a priority, with heavier sentences for anyone soliciting or using the services of a prostitute. There are all sorts of provisions, wider powers for the police and a crackdown on corruption."

"This is either a bad joke or we've all time travelled back to medieval times. Surely there is no chance whatsoever of any of this becoming law?"

"Well, Sara, that is an interesting question. Some of the broad principles of this bill were mentioned in the party's manifesto and enthusiastically accepted by the electorate. Certainly, the measures proposed go much further than anyone outside the party expected, but the Government does not have to face another general election for five years and has a massive majority in the House of Commons. Today has also seen the publication of the bill to abolish the House of Lords. Should that house cease to exist, then it is hard to see who can stop this bill becoming law."

"Can the king refuse to pass this into law?"

"In theory, yes, but King Charles has followed his mother's belief that the monarchy should not influence the political course of the nation. Before he became king, I am certain he would have had a lot to say about this, but in his present role, I would consider it extremely unlikely that he will oppose measures that the public have supported in huge numbers at the ballot box."

"You mentioned that vaginal sex is only permitted within marriage. Does this include established partnerships who have not actually tied the knot?"

"My understanding of this is that marriage means couples who have a marriage certificate issued either by a religious establishment or a registry office. May I look forward to a wedding invitation soon then, Sara?"

"We hear too much about human rights sometimes, but surely it is a basic human right to live your private and sex life however you wish, providing you aren't clearly breaking the law by, for example, sleeping with a child?"

"If this bill is passed, you will be breaking the law if you have vaginal sex whilst you are unmarried or if you practise same-gender sex."

"I need a break to digest all this. I must say I have never been so shaken by a piece of legislation in my life. When we return, I will start to speak to people who, I suspect, will be as stunned by all this as I am, beginning with the former joint leader of the Common Sense Party, David McDougall. See you in a few minutes."

Once off air, Sara demands a strong drink and issues a string of expletives with Bob Godwin's name intertwined with the swear words.

*

In the break, an exhausted-looking David McDougall sits alongside Sara.

"You look terrible," Sara says to her old friend.

"Thanks a lot," David replies ruefully. "It's been a tough forty-eight hours."

"I'm going to ask you why you are not our prime minister or indeed any kind of minister. Is that okay?"

"Yes, Sara, that is more than okay. I have quite a lot to say about how the party has thrown me to the wolves as well."

"Right, we'll start with why Bob Godwin is in charge of everything now."

"Thirty seconds to air," the voice in Sara's ear advises her. "Fifteen seconds. Five, four, three, two, on air."

"Hello and welcome back to *The Sara Molan Politics Show*. As promised before the break, I am now joined by David McDougall, a familiar face to all of you, and until very recently, joint leader of the Common Sense Party. David, when Common Sense won the general election, most of us expected you to be prime minister or at least a senior minister. From your viewpoint, what has happened?"

"Well, Sara, it was agreed that I would front the general election campaign due to my media experience, and if we were successful, then the executive committee would decide whether there would be joint leaders or just one person in charge. After the general election, I came back to Westminster from my constituency and found that Bob Godwin had taken charge of everything. Now I hear I'm not even getting a minister's job. I founded this party, and I am completely pissed off at the way I'm being treated."

"Now, David, you know better than to use language like that," Sara says sternly. "I must apologise to any viewers offended by the language used by my guest in the heat of the moment."

"Yes, I'm sorry. It's just a shock to be on the outside of something I've worked on for so long."

"What has Mr Godwin said to you?"

"Absolutely nothing. He's gone into seclusion and is just firing off his crazy plans and instructions from inside a locked office. It's ludicrous. I mean even Donald Trump knew how to use modern communications. I'm expecting carrier pigeons to bring his next set of commandments to the populous."

Sara laughs nervously, but she carries on with the interview. "What do you think of the justice bill? Common Sense campaigned on law and order, so tightening up the laws and increasing punishments can hardly be a surprise to you?"

"It's absolutely crazy. I made it clear that if we won the general election, punishments would be increased and the death penalty would be introduced for all murders. That is what the majority of our citizens want, but forming a firing squad to shoot people down in cold blood… *It beggars belief.*" David's voice rises considerably during the last few words, resulting in him appearing to be shouting uncontrollably at the expressionless Sara.

"You seem to be very agitated about all this."

"Agitated! I am bloody furious. This was not supposed to happen. I intended to talk to experts and find the most humane way to carry out the death penalty with dignity and respect. Not lining people up against a wall and tearing them to bits with automatic rifles or some such nonsense. It's barbaric."

"Perhaps we could move on to other aspects of the proposed changes, such as clamping down on unmarried sex, homosexuality and prostitution."

"Yes, well, I'm happily married and planning on staying that way, so I'm not affected by this. A lot of people will be, though. It is no secret that I abhor prostitution, and I certainly support any action to rid society of that blight."

"But what about homosexuality? There is nothing in your party's manifesto about any changes to legislation on same-sex relationships. Yet we're only a few days into a new government, and all homosexual relationships are being turned into criminal acts with the likelihood of imprisonment, flogging and possibly even branding. You told me prior to the general election that none of us had any reason to fear Common Sense. Now all unmarried couples and anyone who is not straight face persecution on the same scale as rapists and paedophiles. I would put it to you, David, that many people today have every right to be afraid of your party."

"Um… well, um, Sara, I'm not sure that it is my party any longer."

"You are, as we speak, an MP representing the Common Sense Party," Sara states firmly.

"Yes, that's right. I do not support all parts of the justice bill. It is not what I believe is the right way to bring down crime, which is what the electorate wants. Certainly, punishments need to be increased, but I disagree with many of the measures proposed today. I have never been an advocate of government coming into the bedroom. Trying to control people's sex lives is not the role of Parliament and is definitely not something that was ever discussed as possible party policy in my presence."

"Are you saying then, David, that these proposals are coming from the prime minister rather than the party as a whole?"

"What I'm saying is that the justice bill proposed today criminalises acts that were never discussed at any policy or manifesto meetings I attended. Whether this is down to Bob, the executive committee or some coven of backers, I have no idea. I will say clearly, though, that I am shocked and disgusted at some of the proposals made today and also at the complete lack of communication by the prime minister and the relevant ministers. There have been no press conferences, TV interviews or even statements to the house by any senior official since the day after the general election. All we get is a spokesperson reading out Mr Godwin's missives, like a herald during the Roman Empire. It is wrong, and I will do everything I can to change things."

"Are you going to vote against the justice bill?"

"You must understand that I have only heard what you have heard: the bare bones of a complex piece of legislation. As always with these matters, the devil is in the detail. I need to see the entire bill and work out which parts I can support and which parts I cannot support. I am certainly prepared to vote against those elements I will never feel able to support."

"The problem is, though, that the prime minister holds a huge majority in the House of Commons. The

House of Lords is certain to be abolished. Mr Godwin can do what he likes, can't he?"

David McDougall shuffles uncomfortably in his chair and takes a sip of water before answering. "I know all of my newly elected party colleagues. The vast majority of them are God-fearing, sensible people who I believe have no wish to criminalise the day-to-day activities of millions of their constituents. I have made my position clear in that I will oppose any legislation I do not feel is the right way forward for our four great countries. I am confident many MPs on my own side of the house, along with the opposition parties, will join me in defeating anything that is inhumane or threatens democracy as we now know it."

"So, you will oppose your own party."

"I do not feel able to support the use of firing squads, for instance. It is inhumane to an unbelievable degree. As I have just said, I will try as hard as possible to oppose the clauses of the bill that I disagree with."

"David, let's get a clear answer to this. Will you or will you not vote against your own party if you disagree with their proposals?"

"Yes, but only if I feel strongly that the proposition is wrong."

"Right, we'll wrap today's programme up there. Thank you very much, David McDougall, for being my special guest today, and I hope you can all join me at the same time tomorrow. Goodbye from all the team here. Goodbye."

Once off air, David sighs heavily and, addressing Sara, says, "God, it's harder on this side of the desk. Who turned you into a tigress? I thought you were one of the gentle ones."

"Well, if you will go into politics, this is what you get. I'm sorry I had to push you, but you've already learned the politician's trump card of not answering the question. Look, you need some sleep, but you've got my number if you want a drink or an off-the-record chat. I'm relying on you to overturn this damn bill. Nic and I really aren't in a position to marry."

"I'll see what I can do. Look after yourself, Sara. There are almost as many bastards in this studio as there are in the house."

CHAPTER 2

LEANNE AND LIAM

MAY 2029 – NOVEMBER 2029

Leanne Hervey is sixteen years old, lives with her parents in Ashby-de-la-Zouch, Leicestershire, and is studying for her exams at the local academy. She is blonde, petite and a gifted athlete.

Liam Jones is nineteen and something of a bad boy, although undeniably attractive to teenage girls. He is an apprentice at a manufacturing company that is also based in Ashby-de-la-Zouch. For the last few months, he has been sharing Leanne's bedroom at her parents' house, despite her parents' concerns that he is three years older than his girlfriend.

On 1st July 2029, the happy couple spend the evening listening to music in Leanne's bedroom whilst her parents watch TV downstairs. Just after midnight, Leanne and Liam go to bed and make love. They are still in each other's arms when their bedroom door is forcibly opened, and three police officers burst in.

"*Stay just where you are,*" shouts one of the policemen as the naked lovebirds break apart and dive under the duvet for privacy.

"What the hell is going on?" asks Mr Hervey as he tries to enter his daughter's room.

"Would you please go back to your room, sir," orders the one female police officer. "We will come and talk to you shortly." Turning back to Leanne and Liam she adds, "You are both under arrest on suspicion of having vaginal sex whilst unmarried. Will you please get dressed, and then we will take you both to the police station to question you about this matter."

With neither teenager responding, and Leanne starting to cry, the officer states, "Come on, get some clothes on or I'll charge you with resisting arrest as well."

Liam seems close to tears as he says, "We will when you all leave the room."

"Not a chance, sonny," responds one of the male officers. "Out of bed now."

Both Leanne and Liam try to cover themselves up as much as possible as the two male officers openly ogle Leanne's slim body. Once dressed, the two youngsters are taken outside and put in separate police cars for the trip to Ashby-de-la-Zouch police station. The female officer goes to speak to Mr and Mrs Hervey and informs them that they may be charged with aiding and abetting their daughter and her boyfriend engaging in premarital sex.

*

At the police station, Leanne and Liam are questioned separately, and the police discover that their sexual relationship began when Leanne was aged fifteen and, therefore, below the age of consent. Liam is charged with having sex whilst unmarried and having sex with a minor. Leanne is charged with having sex whilst unmarried, having sex whilst under the legal age of consent and with being a slut. All charges are brought under the Justice Act 2029.

*

A few days later, Liam and Leanne each receive a summons to appear in court on Wednesday, 11th July. Mr and Mrs Hervey also receive letters advising that they are to appear in court on the same date, being accused of allowing an illegal sexual relationship to take place at their property.

*

On arrival at court, they have to push through a number of reporters, who are covering one of the first sex offences trials under the new Justice Act. They are all placed in separate cells awaiting their hearings.

Leanne is the first to appear in court.

The clerk of the court asks her to stand up in the dock. Once she has done so, the clerk asks whether she pleads guilty or not guilty.

Leanne is close to tears as she quietly answers, "Guilty." She is then told to sit down in the dock.

The prosecution counsel then stands and outlines the facts of the case: "The defendant willingly entered into a sexual relationship with her boyfriend when she was aged just fifteen. This relationship continued over several months until the police were tipped off and, consequently, raided the house of the defendant's parents. The defendant was found in her own bed with her boyfriend, Liam Jones. She subsequently admitted to having a sexual relationship that began when she was under the age of consent, and she also stated that she and Liam were not married. She has been charged with being a slut, as it is obvious that her behaviour at such a young age is highly promiscuous and offensive to all decent people. I ask you, Your Honour, to hand down a sentence of immediate detention, severe corporal punishment and branding for this defendant, to serve as a deterrent to her and all other young women. This kind of behaviour is illegal now under our present government, as well as being socially reprehensible."

Leanne starts crying uncontrollably as members of the public gasp at the strong words they have just heard.

Leanne's solicitor, Paul Briscoe rises. He states, "Your Honour, the picture my learned colleague paints of my client could not be further from the truth. She is a respectable young lady who is doing very well at school. This is not a sordid affair. She has a boyfriend whom she is deeply in love with. They have plans to settle down together, marry when they are older and, hopefully, raise a family together. Her boyfriend is her only sexual partner, and their relationship has not been carried out in the back seats of cars or on park benches late at night. No, it has been conducted in her family's home with the full knowledge of her parents. My client is as far away from anyone's image of a slut as it is possible to imagine. Leanne has pleaded guilty on my advice because, technically, she has committed an offence under the newly introduced Justice Act, and she did start sexual activity a few months before the legal age of consent. Under the current legislation, she is automatically considered to be a slut in the eyes of the law as she was underage when commencing a sexual relationship. Despite my learned colleague's strong comments, I believe that Leanne's offences are deserving of punishment at the lower end of the scale. Liam is her only sexual partner, she is immature and to some extent under the influence of an older partner. She has a promising future ahead of her. I ask the court to look leniently upon my client, who is most unlikely to offend in future. Thank you, Your Honour."

The judge immediately orders Leanne to stand up in the dock. She does so, sobbing quietly.

"The defendant has pleaded guilty to very serious offences," the judge concludes sternly. "I have listened carefully to the mitigation presented by Mr Briscoe and I accept that his client is young and may have been pressurised by her older, more experienced boyfriend. However, there is no disputing the facts. The defendant entered into a consensual sexual relationship whilst underage. The sexual activity has continued beyond her sixteenth birthday when she could have married with her parents' consent and at least legitimised the latter part of the relationship. These two actions clearly show her, in both my view and the law's, to be a slut."

The judge pauses as Leanne's sobs become louder and more frequent, before continuing, "It is no good crying. You have brought this entirely upon yourself. I sentence you to twelve months' youth detention, and a total of 250 strokes of the cane on your bare buttocks, 250 strokes of the cane on your bare breasts and 500 strokes of a nine-tailed whip on your bare back. I will leave it in the hands of the regional punishment centre to decide over how many sessions the sentence will be carried out. I additionally sentence you to be branded on your forehead as a slut. It is a provision of this punishment that you are not allowed to cover this branding with hair, a hat or any item of clothing for the rest of your life. Take the prisoner down."

Two court officials grab Leanne's arms and lead her down the steps to the cells. She is barely aware of what is happening. She can hear someone crying hysterically and, slowly, realises that it is herself. She is placed, still upset, into a cell and hears someone say, "You'll stay here until the van arrives to take you to the youth detention centre. They will soon give you something to cry about."

*

Liam Jones pleads guilty to having sex whilst unmarried and to having sex with a minor. He is sentenced to two years' imprisonment, 500 strokes of the cane on his bare buttocks, 500 strokes of the nine-tailed whip on his bare back and branding as a paedophile.

*

Mr and Mrs Hervey plead not guilty to allowing an illegal sexual relationship to take place on their premises, but they are both found guilty by the judge. They are each sentenced to 100 strokes of the cane on their bare buttocks. Due to their daughter and her boyfriend being detained, Mr and Mrs Hervey are the only defendants left to face the rugby scrum of reporters outside the court, and express horror at the severity of the sentences.

Mr Hervey tells a reporter, "We will definitely be voting Conservative in future."

*

The next morning, the case is all over the national newspapers. After reading of Leanne's fate at home on her day off, Sara Molan speaks to her partner on the phone. "Well, if we aren't going to get married, then I don't see how we have a future. I am not going to let that bastard in Number Ten have me jailed, flogged and branded just because I enjoy sex," she says.

"How about going abroad where we can do what we like?" replies Nic.

"I've battled sexism and racism for eight years to get to my present job. I'm not giving that up for anyone."

"Including me, apparently," snaps Nic irritably.

"Especially you," comes the stark reply.

"*Sod you then,*" shouts Nic, slamming down the phone.

"Sod you too," replies Sara to the dialling tone. It is fully thirty seconds before she collapses on her sofa, crying uncontrollably and hurling her engagement ring at the wall.

GOVERNMENT PRONOUNCEMENTS

During the first six months' tenure of this government, no ministers give interviews or personally release any official statements. Government spokesperson Andrew Forrester makes official videos, known as "government pronouncements", which are released to all registered media outlets.

In this opening period of control by the Common Sense Party, the following policies are introduced to the British public by Mr Forrester:

July 2029: David McDougall is expelled from the Common Sense Party for unhelpful comments following a series of interviews calling for moderation from the Government. All school pupils committing crimes at their schools may choose whether to be punished by their school or tried in a court.

August 2029: All convicted sex offenders are to receive at least 500 strokes of the nine-tailed whip. All convicted male rapists are to be castrated. All convicted rapists are to be sentenced to life imprisonment.

September 2029: Crime is down 12% since the general election, but there has been a big increase in sex offences, so additional strengthening of the law in that area is being considered.

October 2029: All schoolgirls in full-time education who are aged eleven and over are to be given virginity tests annually. Every member of the public who has knowledge of illegal sexual relationships, including those between unmarried partners, must report that information to the police. Failure to do so will be a criminal offence carrying a minimum punishment of three months' imprisonment and 500 strokes of the nine-tailed whip.

CHAPTER 3

PAUL

NOVEMBER 2029 – MAY 2030

Paul Taylor is twenty-nine years old, is of ethnic origin, is married and has two children, one aged three years and the other aged one year.

At the start of the second six months of the Common Sense Party's first government, Paul is walking home from work. It is a dark, rainy night, and he is hurrying to get home to his family. Paul passes a car parked at the side of the road. As he moves past this vehicle, its car alarm goes off. There is no one else around, and knowing that he did not touch the car, Paul keeps walking. About 100 yards further on, he is stopped by the car's owner, who accuses him of damaging the vehicle.

The police are called and, apparently, find a scratch on the side of the car nearest to the pavement Paul was walking on. Paul is taken to the police station and charged with criminal damage. Paul pleads his innocence.

*

Just three days after his arrest, he is summarily sacked from his job. When Paul attempts to claim benefits, he is told it is his own fault that he is unemployed. With money now tight, Paul cannot afford a solicitor, so he has no choice but to represent himself in court. He is found guilty and sentenced to two months' imprisonment and 300 strokes of the cane on his bare buttocks. He is also ordered to pay compensation to the car owner for the damage caused.

It probably means nothing, but the car owner and the arresting police officer are seen later on the day of Paul's trial drinking together in a pub near the courthouse.

Paul is taken to the newly built Stenfield Prison and medically examined before being given his uniform. He is then put in a cell with convicted burglar Andy Matthews. The next few days pass quietly with Andy taking his new cellmate under his wing and introducing Paul to prison routine.

*

On the sixth day of Paul's sentence, another prisoner named Mark O'Rourke enters the cell and tells Andy to get lost.

"Got any fags?" asks O'Rourke in a tone that makes it seem far more of a demand than a simple question.

"No," replies Paul. "I don't smoke."

"Well, you'd better have some tomorrow when I come around. Remember, your kind do not fit in around here, so you need protection from someone like me, and that will cost you. We don't want you getting hurt, do we?"

"I can look after myself," Paul responds, trying to sound more confident than he feels.

"Oh, you think so, do you?"

As he speaks, O'Rourke moves forwards suddenly and punches Paul in the stomach. Without thinking, Paul responds in kind, sending a right-hand punch straight into his opponent's face.

With blood gushing from his nose, O'Rourke departs, shouting, "*You are going to regret this.*"

Andy returns immediately and asks, "What the hell did you do that for? Just give him a few fags, and we will all have a nice quiet life."

"I didn't have any fags, and anyway, he hit me first," Paul explains.

"Like that matters in here. I would have given you some fags to tide him…" Andy's words trail off as two warders appear in the doorway of the cell.

"Matthews, make yourself scarce," says one of the officers.

"Yes, sir." Andy can hardly get out of the cell quickly enough.

"Right, Taylor," continues the officer. "I've got a prisoner with a bloody nose who says you hit him for no reason."

"He was demanding fags, and when I said no, he hit me first – in the stomach," Paul replies as calmly as he can. "Also, he made a racist remark."

"What a pity," states the warder, and then turning to his colleague, instructs, "Let's get him into solitary and then ask the governor whether he wants to deal with this or refer it to the police."

His colleague laughs and offers, "I think I know which it will be if it's up to the great buck-passer to decide."

Paul is half dragged out of the cell and moved to a different floor of the prison, where he is placed in a bare, small room with a bench, a bunk and a bucket. "All mod cons in here." The officer laughs. "No TVs and snooker tables nowadays, thanks to good ol' Bob Godwin."

They depart, and Paul is left with his thoughts.

About three hours later, a different prison warder unlocks the cell and tells Paul that the governor has referred the matter to the local police, who will interview him and decide whether he will be charged. In the meantime, Paul is to stay in his luxury individual accommodation.

*

The next day, Staffordshire Police charge Paul with actual bodily harm, and he is transferred to Exeter Prison in Devon to prevent him launching further attacks on Mark O'Rourke or anyone else in Stenfield.

*

Three weeks later, Paul appears in court via a video link. Mark O'Rourke denies under oath that he hit Paul during their "discussion" about cigarettes. Paul tries to put his case across, but a recurring fault on the video line means many of his words are not heard in the court. The judge finds Paul guilty of assault causing actual bodily harm. He is sentenced to a further eighteen months imprisonment and 500 strokes of the nine-tailed whip.

*

The following Wednesday, Paul is taken – totally without warning – to Plymouth to attend the regional punishment centre. He is placed in handcuffs and accompanied by two guards. He receives 150 strokes of the cane and 250 strokes of the nine-tailed whip – half of his total sentence. Bleeding and in extreme pain, he is given no medical assistance at all, either at the centre or back at the prison.

That night he sleeps naked and face down for the first of many times. At least, on this occasion, he's in a single cell.

PAUL

*

The Friday of that week brings the first visitors' day since Paul was transferred to Exeter. He is expecting a visit from his wife, Darlene, but they both face major logistical problems in order to be together. Paul must somehow put on his prison uniform just forty-eight hours after receiving his brutal corporal punishment. His wife faces a lengthy, difficult journey by bus and train to visit him.

They are both somewhat fraught when they sit down, one each side of a big plastic screen in the communal visiting room.

"You look awful," remarks Darlene, somewhat shocked by her husband's pale, drawn face and his wincing as he sits on his chair.

"I got the first half of my punishment strokes on Wednesday," Paul replies, trying to sound cheerful. "I'll be fine in a day or two."

"I really can't believe you were stupid enough to get in a fight. How am I supposed to cope for another eighteen bloody months?"

"Yeah, well life isn't exactly a bunch of roses from this side of the screen either, you know."

"You've changed. I don't want my kids brought up with a violent thug."

"What the hell are you talking about?" questions Paul.

"I'm filing for divorce, and I shall be seeking sole custody of the children," Darlene replies icily.

"You are not taking my kids away from me," shouts Paul.

This causes the duty officer to respond: "That's enough, Taylor. One more outburst and you're on report and back in your cell."

"What do you expect me to do?" asks Darlene. "You always told me to turn the other cheek whenever anyone made remarks about the colour of my skin or when life kicked us in the teeth. We were already in a mess before you scratched that car. If that wasn't enough, you break someone's nose because he wants a cigarette and give us all another eighteen months of hell. Never mind your sore back; you want to try telling a three-year-old there's nothing for tea or explain why he can't have a new toy car." Darlene is in tears by the end of these comments.

"None of this is my fault, Darlene," defends Paul, trying to keep his voice as quiet as possible. "You've got to believe me. I never touched that car; I was stitched up. And I didn't start that fight."

"It's never your fault, is it? Well, you can't blame me this time. Face it, Paul, you're just the same as everyone else in here. A violent, no-good chancer putting the blame on anyone within sight. It's over, Paul. I'm going ahead with the divorce whether you like it or not."

Darlene gets up to go as Paul jumps up from his chair screaming, *"You can't do this to me. Darlene, please. Not the children. Darlene."*

At this point, he is unceremoniously grabbed by two prison officers and forced down onto the ground.

A sobbing Darlene leaves the visiting room without a backwards glance.

"Solitary for you and up before the governor tomorrow. You must love being flogged to do this just forty-eight hours after the last lot," suggests one of the officers as they march Paul, still screaming his wife's name, to a punishment cell clearly designed by the same person who created the rooms at Stenfield.

*

With much more severe prison regimes introduced by the new government, the prison governor has no hesitation in sentencing Paul to be flogged 250 times with a bullwhip and to serve a further six months in prison.

*

Sara Molan arrives at the TV studios to find a large bouquet of flowers waiting for her. Surprised, she finds the attached card and reads the message: "To Sara, with love from Bob." Still confused, she phones the florists and asks if they can tell her who sent the flowers.

The florist replies, "We don't have a specific name, but the request came from the prime minister's office."

Sara puts down the phone, snorts and throws the flowers in a bin. She wishes briefly that the name on the card had been "Nic", but she soon concentrates on preparing herself for her forthcoming daily programme and her latest interview with her former colleague David McDougall.

A few minutes later, Sara is back to her normal "couldn't care less" calmness as she introduces David to her unseen audience: "Today's guest is no stranger to this studio, but he is now dipping his toe into even murkier waters as an independent MP following him losing the government whip. Please welcome David McDougall. David, this is the first time we have spoken since you left Common Sense. Would you describe the parting of the ways as amicable or very difficult?"

"Well, Sara, from my point of view, I think it was regretful. The prime minister appears to be running a one-man band and refuses to listen to anyone. It is no secret that I find many of the recent pronouncements, as we have to call them, ridiculously severe. The witch hunt against women, schoolgirls and the nation's private lives is not the way to reduce proper crime. It is cruel, barbaric and ruining people's lives. We have women being branded for life, flogged and imprisoned just for having sex. I have consistently voted against these savage proposals, and I believe that my opposition to virginity tests in secondary schools was the final straw for our reclusive prime minister. I am proud to sit in Parliament as an independent MP, voting according to my conscience and not as a mere puppet of a regime that seems to want to take us back to the Dark Ages."

"Those are very strong words, considering that you helped to draw up the Government's law and order policy."

"I drew up a sensible, structured way to reduce crime, concentrating on the increased use of prison sentences to cut down burglary, antisocial behaviour and domestic abuse in particular for the first two or three years. Read the manifesto; there is nothing in there about criminalising sex and flogging people half to death."

"You did, however, propose to reintroduce capital punishment for all murders."

"Yes, Sara, I did. But as I have said many times, it was my intention to use the most humane methods possible, not provide target practice for our armed forces."

"Coming back to your departure from Common Sense, what did the prime minister say to you?"

"Sweet FA as usual. He doesn't speak to anyone apart from his personal waiter. He just fires out memos and pronouncements. You need to get him on this programme and interrogate him about what he is doing to this fine nation."

"We have tried, but we never get any meaningful response. We did ask him to come on and discuss your concerns face to face, but he did not reply."

"I will state publicly here and now that I will debate my concerns with the prime minister anywhere and at any time. Come on, Bob, meet me face to face and explain why you are maiming people because of their sex lives. Tell us why you are subjecting eleven-year-olds to virginity tests, which experts say are inaccurate and cause unnecessary distress. Please explain to me and the electorate why you are using firing squads to carry out death sentences."

"We will certainly pass your suggestion of a face-to-face meeting on to Downing Street and see what their response is."

"Don't hold your breath."

"Right, on that note, we will take a short break, and when we come back, I will be discussing with several different guests how they see our current relationship with what is left of the EU."

"Sara, very quickly, may I say that if anyone viewing is unhappy with the Government's decisions, would they please write to me, David McDougall MP, care of the House of Commons."

"I'll see you after the break," Sara says to the audience.

She then turns to David as the ad break starts and states, "That went very well, I think. Great TV, and you never know, we might even shake a certain someone off his golden perch. You take care, though, David; it's much harder to beat an invisible enemy."

David replies, "If anyone can get an interview with Godwin, it's you."

*

After completing the rest of the programme, Sara returns to her dressing room and, with a sigh, retrieves the flowers from the bin. She then dials a number on her mobile phone. "Hello. Yes, may I speak to the prime minister, please?"

"I'm afraid he's in a meeting at the moment and cannot be disturbed. May I give him a message?" replies the person who answered the call.

"Mmm. Yes. Um, my name is Sara Molan. I want to thank him for the flowers, and could he ring me, please? He should have my number."

GOVERNMENT PRONOUNCEMENTS

November 2029: All unmarried women are to be virginity tested annually. In view of this, before the end of January 2030, any unmarried woman who has been in a sexual relationship prior to May 2029 must provide the police with full details of her sexual partners and the start and finish dates of the relationship. Failure to do so will leave individuals open to prosecution for offences relating to these relationships when they fail a virginity test for the first time.

January 2030: Oral and anal sex are banned for all unmarried citizens.

February 2030: All women convicted of rape or assisting in rape will undergo a total hysterectomy as well as mandatory imprisonment and corporal punishment. Any person who claims to be the victim of rape, attempted rape or sexual assault will be automatically guilty of making false accusations of abuse if any or all of the accused are acquitted. The minimum punishment will be a total of 500 strokes of the nine-tailed whip.

March 2030: All convicted male paedophiles are to be castrated. All convicted female paedophiles are to be sentenced to undergo a total hysterectomy.

May 2030: Crime rates have gone down 30% in the last six months. The Government accepts that there is some criticism of its judicial policies, but states it is only doing what it promised and what the electorate voted for. The Government also wishes to repeat its previous message that the prime minister will not be commenting publicly on any policy decisions, but will instead concentrate on running the country and driving crime figures down.

CHAPTER 4

LEAH

MAY 2030 – NOVEMBER 2030

By May 2030, Anne Marshall has been a teacher at Derby Academy for fifteen years. The first Thursday in May is like any other, as she quietly watches the children milling around the playground after lunch. Suddenly, she hears a commotion at the far end of the yard, and as she gets nearer, she can make out a female voice screaming words that she considers most unladylike:

"You fucking well leave him alone, you bitch. He's mine and don't you ever fucking forget it."

Anne is now close enough to see what is happening, and the yelling is followed by a heavy punch from the speaker to her rival. The second girl reels backwards from the punch and lands heavily on the hard concrete surface of the playground.

The assailant, whom Miss Marshall can now identify as sixth-former Leah Stafford, immediately jumps on top of her opponent and continues to punch her whilst shouting things such as, "*I'll rip your fucking head off,*" and, "*You're dead, you scumbag.*"

Several pupils have gathered around, and Anne scatters them by threatening them all with detention if they don't disappear. She also instructs one boy to fetch the school nurse urgently. Miss Marshall then tries to separate the two combatants. This proves easier said than done, as Leah does not intend to give up her advantageous position sitting on top of her rival and is punching her at every opportunity. In the melee, Anne gets an elbow in the face and a punch in the stomach.

The arrival of the nurse, Diane Street, gives Anne the additional resources she needs to finally separate the girls. Miss Marshall pulls the still-ranting Leah away whilst the nurse examines the stricken girl on the floor, who is bleeding profusely from her nose, mouth and the back of her head from where she landed on the surface of the playground.

"What on earth has happened here?" the teacher asks.

"She's been messing with my boyfriend," comes the reply from Leah.

"And that justifies violence, does it? I'm ashamed of you, Stafford. Brawling and injuring a fellow pupil over a boy. Haven't you learned anything in your years here?"

Miss Marshall doesn't wait for a reply to her questions, but addresses the nurse instead. "Diane, how is she?"

"I think we'd better get an ambulance, Anne. The cut on the back of her head is deep, and I can't stop the bleeding at the moment."

As Diane finishes talking, they are joined by the head of the sixth form, David Travers.

"Ah, Mr Travers, this one belongs to you. Would you take charge of Stafford, and I'll get an ambulance for the other one?" suggests Anne.

"That one is Kay Russell. I imagine we've got her emergency contact details on file, so I'll find them, ring her next of kin and give them the good news," declares Mr Travers. "Will you let me know if they take her to hospital?" Turning to the now slightly calmer Leah, he adds, "You realise you are in a lot of trouble, young lady? I am going to have to inform the headmaster and your parents. Come with me."

"I don't care. She deserved it. I hope the little cheat dies in the ambulance," retorts Leah.

"Come on inside, and if I were you, I'd watch what I say," commands Mr Travers.

He takes Leah into the school and decides to deposit her in the school secretary's office whilst he finds out how badly Kay is hurt. He orders Leah to face the office wall, put her hands on her head and not to utter a sound unless she is spoken to. For a second, he finds himself admiring the back of her legs in her shorter-than-permitted uniform skirt and the long, blonde hair hanging over her shoulders and down her back before snapping back to harsh reality.

He then goes back to the playground where Kay Russell is still lying on the ground but now attended by two paramedics. "How is she?" he asks the hovering nurse.

"They are taking her to the hospital, so if possible, can you get her parents to go straight there?"

Mr Travers manages to contact Kay's mother and then goes to see the headmaster, Sir Malcolm Potter.

"A nasty business this," says the headmaster, stroking his chin thoughtfully. "As I understand it, she has the choice now whether to be punished by us or through the courts."

"Yes, that's the current position. If I were her, I wouldn't go anywhere near the courts with all the branding and flogging going on nowadays," replies Mr Travers.

"Well, I think we'll let her contemplate what she has done for an hour or so, and then we can get her in and decide how to deal with this. Will you please inform her parents what has happened?"

"Certainly," agrees Mr Travers as he leaves the room.

The telephone conversation with Mrs Stafford goes reasonably well in the circumstances, although David is unsure whether to pass on to Leah her mother's message, which promises her a sound beating from her father when she gets home.

It is mid-afternoon when Mr Travers returns to the secretary's office after the phone call. Leah is still standing facing the wall.

"Any problems?" he asks the secretary.

"None at all," she replies.

"Right, Stafford, it's time to face the music." With that, he beckons her to follow him out of the office.

Leah and Mr Travers walk the corridor to the headmaster's office. When they arrive, the teacher tells Leah to face the wall again and put her hands on her head. He then knocks and enters the office.

A couple of first-year boys walk past Leah, making comments such as, "You're going to get the cane," and, "What are you doing tonight?"

After what seems like hours to the sixth-former, the office door opens, and Mr Travers tells her to come in. The headmaster is sitting in a large chair behind an enormous desk. Leah walks slowly to the desk, whilst Mr Travers takes up a position on the right side of the office.

"Right, young lady," begins the headmaster in his sternest voice. "I have a fifteen-year-old pupil in hospital with serious injuries to her head and face. I also have a respected teacher telling me she has been elbowed and punched, and you seem to be responsible. What do you have to say for yourself?"

Leah tries to avoid the headmaster's gaze by looking at the carpet.

"Look at me, girl," barks Sir Malcolm.

Leah does so and replies almost in a whisper, "She deserved it. I didn't mean to catch Marshall." The headmaster's glower in her direction makes her pause and reconsider before continuing, "Er, Miss Marshall; she just got in the way. I'm really sorry about that."

"But not about Miss Russell?"

"She's a slag; she got what she deserved."

"That's enough. You're not with your friends now. Watch your language, young lady. Now you have the choice whether you wish me to hand this matter over to the police or deal with it myself. I should tell you that I am far from impressed with your behaviour today, both in the playground and in this office. If you decide to be punished here, then I must advise you that I shall deal with you most severely. Yes, most severely indeed."

Leah starts to cry quietly, but she pulls herself together enough to tell the headmaster she wants to be punished by the school. She is told to wait outside again, which she does.

After a couple of minutes, she is summoned back in.

"Leah Stafford, I am satisfied that you are guilty of assaulting Kay Russell and Miss Marshall today," explains the headmaster. "I also find your attitude and language totally unacceptable, and your skirt is far too short. This is a respectable school, and as a sixth-former, you are expected to behave like an adult, not a first year. You will do one hour's detention every Wednesday until the end of this term. You will also assist the duty teacher every Thursday lunchtime until the end of term. That deals with your rudeness and your skirt. For the assaults you have perpetrated today, I intend to punish you as follows: I am now going to administer 200 strokes of the cane to your bare bottom. Mr Travers will act as a witness. When I've finished speaking, you can inform me if you want anyone else to be present. Tomorrow, you will receive a further 150 strokes at morning assembly in front of the whole school. When Nurse Street tells me that you have recovered from that, I will cane you again 150 times in front of the lower sixth form, of which you are a member, of course. You can count yourself lucky you're not being suspended or expelled."

Leah doesn't feel lucky at all. She is fighting back tears and feeling deeply sorry for herself. She soon realises that the headmaster is waiting for her to respond about a witness. "Why would I need someone else in here?" she asks hesitantly.

"Both Mr Travers and I happen to be male. You are going to be naked when I cane you, and you might wish to choose someone else, possibly female, to be present."

Naked. The word explodes in Leah's head, and she begins to cry heavily.

Mr Travers' voice cuts through the wailing. "Headmaster, I think that someone else should be present to protect ourselves and Leah. If she can't decide, should we ask Miss Marshall to be here, perhaps?"

This suggestion pulls Leah out of her silence. "No, please, not her. I want my boyfriend here."

"I don't think that is appropriate at all," concludes the headmaster.

"All this is his fault. I want him to see what damage he's done," explains Leah.

"But, Stafford, you will be naked. Do you want him to see you in that state?"

"It won't be the first time." Leah sees the shocked look on the headmaster's face. "We've not had sex, so you needn't worry about me failing a virginity test and letting down your precious school again. I'll cooperate if he can be here. Otherwise, I'll fight you every inch of the way, today and tomorrow."

"All right," capitulates Sir Malcolm. "Who is this boyfriend and where is he now?"

"Richard Griffin. He's in the upper sixth. He'll be in the sixth-form common room."

The headmaster picks up his telephone and speaks to his secretary. "Mrs Milne, could you please find an upper sixth pupil, Richard Griffin. He should be in the common room, apparently. Thank you."

A few minutes later, there is a knock on the door, and the secretary brings in an athletic, tall, dark-haired young man.

As Mrs Milne leaves, Richard ignores the headmaster and Mr Travers and instead heads straight for Leah. "Why did you attack Kay? There's nothing going on between us. I told you that," he says, as Leah collapses into his arms and begs him to hold her.

"*That's enough of that,*" bellows the headmaster. "Stafford stand in front of my desk. Mr Griffin, you are here – at your girlfriend's insistence – to witness her caning. You are not here to conduct your unseemly romance. I am very annoyed by your involvement with a fellow pupil. I have no doubt Mr Travers will wish to speak to you about your responsibility to the school as a member of the sixth form. I think, Mr Travers, some extra work and a detention or two might focus Mr Griffin's mind on his education, don't you?"

"Yes, sir," responds Mr Travers.

"Right, let's get on with this. Stafford get undressed completely," orders the headmaster.

"Is this really necessary?" asks Richard.

"Yes, it is. Another word from you and you'll be joining her across the desk," declares the headmaster.

Leah takes off her blazer and tie and puts them on the back of a nearby chair. She hesitates, takes a deep breath and then takes off her white blouse, revealing a lacy, black bra and enough cleavage to make her wish she had put on something less exposing. Next, she takes off and puts down her shoes and socks before her skirt joins them on the chair.

David Travers looks on in amazement as Leah's long legs are revealed in all their glory. He can feel himself becoming aroused as he waits for the next item to be removed.

Leah fumbles with the clasp of her bra and does her best to cover up her breasts as the garment finally comes off.

"Hands by your side," barks Sir Malcolm, resulting in everyone in the room being able to see Leah's ample breasts in their full glory.

Leah's tears increase as she starts to slide her panties down, revealing a dark mound of pubic hair and a beautifully formed bottom, amongst other delights. Leah uses her hands to try to cover her vagina.

"*Do you want extra strokes?*" booms the headmaster.

She reluctantly puts her hands by her side.

David is lost in his fantasies. Richard is torn between admiring his girlfriend's beautiful body and imagining how different her bottom will look at the end of the caning.

Sir Malcolm rises from his chair and takes off his suit jacket before unlocking a cupboard alongside his desk. He picks out a couple of canes before putting one back and swishing his choice through the air.

Leah winces at the sound.

"Stafford lean over the desk and grab the far edge with both hands," the headmaster commands. "If you stand up during the punishment, I will repeat the stroke. Mr Travers, go round the desk and hold her shoulders down, so she doesn't move about too much. Mr Griffin, you can count the strokes. Do not try to miscount or you'll be next."

Leah cannot imagine being less comfortable. She is gripping the desk with all her might, terrified of letting go and getting even more strokes. Mr Travers is pinning her down by the shoulders, resulting in her stomach and breasts being flattened onto the desk's cold, unyielding wood. She has never been caned before, but is fully aware that soon the pain in her bottom will obliterate her present discomfort. She can hear the headmaster swishing the cane and then tapping it gently across her bottom. Then, out of nowhere, she feels a searing pain across the centre of her bottom cheeks. Leah battles to keep her grip on the desk as her whole rear feels like it is on fire. Mr Travers tightens his grip to keep her pinned to the desk. Leah's tears flow freely, and a scream erupts from her mouth.

Somewhere in her agony, she hears Richard call out, "One".

A few seconds later, the whole scene is repeated for the second stroke and then the third.

Eventually, the call of, "Two hundred" rings out.

David Travers releases his hold on the stricken girl. He has been unable to see the damage being inflicted on Leah's buttocks, and he is utterly shocked when he moves round the desk. Her bottom is unrecognisable, criss-crossed with cuts and welts and with several areas where the skin has been broken. Blood is running from a few spots, but the teacher has to admire Sir Malcolm's skill with the cane to inflict this much damage without a greater amount of bleeding.

Richard moves forwards to help his girlfriend rise from the desk. Leah's legs are very shaky, and it takes all her boyfriend's strength to stop her slumping on the floor. Leah is no longer remotely concerned about preserving her modesty, standing in the middle of the headmaster's office with Richard holding her up whilst she cries uncontrollably. It is several minutes before she can even attempt to dress, and even then, she is simply unable to get her panties on over her sore, swollen buttocks.

Richard and David help her to the nurse's office, make their excuses and leave.

Diana Street pulls down Leah's skirt gently and inspects the damage. "Well, I must say that is a really well-thrashed backside. I'll get some cream to rub on it. It'll sting like hell to start with, but it will help the pain and the swelling."

It takes about an hour for Leah to even stop crying and about another hour before she can stand on her own two feet, but wearing her panties is still one step too far.

The nurse rings Leah's mother, and a few minutes later she finally leaves the school – until tomorrow.

*

The journey home is undertaken in silence.

When they arrive, and her mother does speak, it is not really what Leah wants to hear. "Upstairs to your room now, strip off and lie face down until your father gets home."

As she hobbles up the stairs, Leah is thankful she hasn't been told to lie face up and realises she will be sleeping on her stomach for a long time to come.

After an hour or so, Leah hears the front door open and shut, followed by raised voices. Soon afterwards, her bedroom door opens. She turns her head slightly and sees her father standing there with a leather strap in his hands. "Please, Dad, no more; please," she begs.

Her father steps forwards and looks at his daughter's battered backside. "How many are you getting tomorrow?" he asks.

"Three hundred," Leah replies dully.

"Better today than tomorrow then, I reckon. Lie flat."

The first stroke seems to reawaken every painful nerve end in her bottom, and it also sets Leah off crying and screaming again. Her father hits her about twenty times, by which time his daughter is in the same amount of pain as after the headmaster had finished with her earlier in the day.

"I haven't finished with you yet," her father says as he leaves the room.

Her mother visits her later, rubs Leah's bottom with more cream and asks if she wants anything to eat. The answer to that is a weary shake of the head.

"Try to get some sleep if you can. It's a big day tomorrow," states her mother as she departs.

Tomorrow, Leah thinks as she tries to find some kind of comfortable position. *The day when I get caned 300 times whilst naked in front of all my friends.*

*

Sleep has been elusive, but Leah is dozing when her alarm goes off. For a moment, she wonders why she is hurting so badly, and then she remembers all too clearly. She showers, extremely painfully, and puts on her school uniform. Initially, she puts on her shortest skirt, but a look in the mirror shows her that redness and some marks are clearly visible, so she quickly changes to a longer version. Putting on her panties proves impossible again, so she leaves them on her chair.

Normally, on Leah's walk to school she picks up Richard halfway, kissing and smooching with him until they are within sight of school. Today, though, her mother is driving her in. Mrs Milne, the headmaster's secretary, is waiting for them when they arrive and she takes charge of the schoolgirl. Leah is soon in Mrs Milne's office, her face pressed to the wall. Too soon, Nurse Street comes to fetch her.

In the nurse's room, Diana tells Leah to undress and then examines the schoolgirl's swollen, red buttocks. "How many are you getting today?"

"Three hundred," is the sad reply.

"I don't think you'll be able to take that many. You're very badly marked up."

"Please, please, don't stop it. I just want it over and done with. I'll get through it; I've got to."

"All right, but if I say you've had enough, then it stops. Understood?"

"Okay, but only if I'm unconscious or struggling to breathe," Leah answers determinedly.

"Let's get you to the hall before the whole school starts heading there."

Even so, many of the school's pupils sneak a quick look at the naked seventeen-year-old limping over to the hall to be the assembly's star attraction. Diana Street takes Leah to the side of the stage, out of sight of the vast majority of the pupils, as the headmaster leads the school through hymns, prayers and Bible readings.

Sir Malcolm then addresses the assembly: "Yesterday, a serious incident occurred in the school playground, which has resulted in a fifth-year student being taken to hospital. I am pleased to report that the pupil concerned has been released and will suffer no permanent injury. However, that does not excuse the behaviour of the person responsible for this unfortunate matter. Discipline has been increased under our new government, something I support wholeheartedly. I want every one of you to remember what is going to happen here today and think back to this morning whenever you are about to do something stupid. I promise every one of you that I shall not hesitate to repeat this severity of punishment whenever I consider it is deserved." He then turns to the two women waiting in the wings and beckons them forwards. There are many gasps as Leah steps into view completely naked and even louder gasps as some of the audience begin to see her bottom.

Tears are welling up in Leah's eyes as she approaches the headmaster. She notices for the first time that a classroom table has been placed on the stage and she is almost relieved when she is told to bend over it. At least the front of her body is no longer fully visible. Diana Street seems to have been delegated both to keep Leah in position and to count the strokes.

For Leah, nothing is really different to the previous day, apart from the larger audience. Each stroke hurts like hell. She cries throughout and screams at each new assault on her buttocks. Nurse Street stops the punishment after fifty and 100 strokes, but allows the headmaster to continue each time. Leah feels a little better as the count enters the 140s and breathes a deep sigh of relief as the final stroke is administered.

She is made to stay across the table until all the pupils have departed. Diana has to grab her when it is finally time to stand up, as Leah's legs buckle as soon as they are required to work. David Travers helps the nurse take Leah back to the sick room. Fortunately, all the students are in class, so further embarrassment is kept to a minimum.

Leah spends the rest of the morning recovering, with regular applications of soothing cream. At lunchtime, the nurse is asked to go to the headmaster's office. Leah begs her not to stop the final instalment of the punishment.

On Diana's return, she says to Leah. "I honestly don't know whether this is the right decision or not, but you're going to get caned again at 2pm in the lower-sixth common room."

*

Just before 2pm, Diana asks Leah if she thinks she can get her shoes, skirt and blouse on to give her some degree of modesty on the walk to the common room. Leah manages to do so, which at least prevents her being seen naked again by the many students moving between lessons at that time.

On arrival, Leah is surprised by the low number of her fellow students in attendance. None of her friends are present in an unexpected, if potentially risky, show of solidarity. However, the headmaster is there, cane in hand. Leah slowly and painfully removes her skirt and blouse, and she bends over a table placed at the front of the room. For the third time in twenty-four hours, she suffers intolerable pain as Sir Malcolm slams the cane down on her buttocks another 150 times, and then, finally, it is over.

Leah dresses again and makes the slow, painful journey back to the sick bay to receive yet more soothing cream and wait for her mother to take her home.

*

Her parents insist that Leah attends school despite her injuries, and it is nearly three weeks before she can sit through a whole lesson comfortably. Richard does not contact her at school or at home, but he does visit Kay Russell at her home several times over the next few weeks. When Kay reappears at school, she is arm in arm with Richard and sporting what appears to be an engagement ring on the third finger of her left hand.

Leah is left with nothing but bittersweet memories, sore buttocks, extra duties and a pile of detentions to get through.

GOVERNMENT PRONOUNCEMENTS

July 2030: Crime is down 38%, but traffic offences are increasing sharply, so stiffer penalties are necessary. All parking and traffic offences are to carry a minimum mandatory punishment of at least six months imprisonment and a two-year driving ban, plus optional fines and corporal punishment.

CHAPTER 5

AARON

NOVEMBER 2030 – MAY 2031

Nobody could ever say that Aaron Davis had an easy childhood. Born prematurely, he suffered brain damage at birth, leaving him with learning difficulties. His father left home before Aaron reached his first birthday, and his mother became increasingly less interested in her son and more interested in alcohol, drugs and having a good time. Aaron was taken into care at five years old and disappeared into the social services equivalent of a black hole, moving uneasily through a lengthy succession of foster homes, institutions and special schools. By his mid-teens, Aaron had a number of juvenile convictions for assault, theft, criminal damage and possession of a knife. After finishing his education with no qualifications, at nineteen years of age, Aaron quickly found himself on the street, unemployed, and increasingly surviving on alcohol and progressively harder drugs.

On 1st November 2030, Aaron tries to buy some cocaine from his dealer, Mikey. Unfortunately, Aaron does not have enough money, and Mikey's response to Aaron's pleas to pay him later is to punch him in the face and leave him crying on the pavement. Aaron wanders around the cold streets for an hour or so, feeling gradually less well and even more desperate for his next fix. Eventually, he waits outside Patel's corner shop and starts harassing customers for money. When that fails, in desperation, he goes into the shop. At first, he simply asks the shopkeeper, Mr Asif Patel, to lend him money. The conversation soon becomes heated, and in a moment of desperation, Aaron pulls a knife out of his jeans pocket and again demands money. Mr Patel tries to grab Aaron's arm and is pushed away. Aaron then stabs the shopkeeper twice before grabbing money from the till and running outside still holding the knife.

Unfortunately for Aaron, a number of people see him running from the shop holding money and a knife. At least two witnesses know Aaron by name. The police and ambulance crew are quickly on the scene.

Aaron is arrested in a nearby park, muttering to himself and still holding both the knife and the cash. He puts down the knife calmly and is arrested, but he reacts violently when officers try to take the money from his grasp.

Mr Patel is rushed to hospital but dies of his injuries that evening.

Aaron is remanded to a psychiatric hospital for his own safety, and the court appoints a barrister (Mr Anthony Jackson KC [King's Counsel]) and a solicitor (Ms Linda Hodgson) to represent him at trial.

In January 2031, Aaron appears at the Old Bailey. He is charged with the murder of Mr Asif Patel on 1st November 2030, the theft of £108.93 belonging to Mr Asif Patel, and the possession of a bladed object, namely a kitchen knife. Aaron is asked to plead, but he doesn't answer. Mr Jackson asks the court to adjourn the hearing for assessment of whether Aaron is fit to plead and stand trial.

Judge Menzies, however, asks Aaron whether he stabbed Mr Patel.

Aaron replies, "Yes."

"And did you steal money from Mr Patel's shop?" the judge continues.

"I object," interrupts Mr Jackson. "This is unfair. He does not understand the implications of what you are asking."

"Overruled. Mr Davis, do you understand what I am asking you? Did you take money from Mr Patel's shop after you stabbed him?" the judge asks again.

"Yes, I did," confirms Aaron.

"Finally, Mr Davis did you have a kitchen knife with you when you entered Mr Patel's shop."

"Yes. I borrowed it when I was in a foster home one time. I keep it to cut up food people give me."

"Your Honour, I object most strongly to this," Mr Jackson says as he rises to his feet. "We must have expert testimony on what my client does and does not understand before we can begin to ascertain his ability to answer questions. My client suffered brain damage at birth. He has considerable learning difficulties. The court needs to hear a professional assessment of those before proceeding any further."

"I disagree entirely, Mr Jackson," remonstrates the judge. "In my opinion the defendant understands perfectly well. With people of limited intelligence, all you need to do is speak slowly and use simple words. How can you argue he does not understand when he not only knows what a knife is but also where he came by it and what it is used for? Objection overruled. On the evidence of the answers given by the defendant to my questions, the court will enter formal pleas of guilty."

"Your Honour!"

"Sit down now, Mr Jackson, before I hold you in contempt. The defendant is remanded into custody for sentencing in twenty-eight days' time. Normal assessment reports are to be carried out."

Ms Hodgson now rises to her feet. "Your Honour, my client is presently being held in a secure psychiatric hospital. I would ask that he be remanded back to that hospital and that the doctors there should carry out the assessments."

"Yes, agreed. The defendant is remanded into psychiatric care as previously. This case is adjourned pending sentencing."

AARON

*

Four weeks later, the cast of this judicial drama appear again in the same courtroom at the Old Bailey. Aaron Davis is dishevelled and appears confused by his surroundings. He mutters to himself constantly and ignores the usher's order for everyone to stand as Judge Menzies enters the court.

"All sit," states the usher.

At that point, Aaron gets up and is quickly seated again by the court official guarding the dock.

The prosecutor, Mr Rhys Evans KC, rises. "Your Honour, the case before us today is a sentencing hearing for the defendant Mr Aaron Davis of no fixed—"

"*That's me*," shouts Aaron from the dock, before being firmly told to shush by the court official.

Judge Menzies interrupts now: "Mr Davis, you are in a courtroom. You are not to speak unless you are spoken to first. Do you understand?"

"No," replies Aaron firmly.

"Would both counsels please approach my bench."

The two comply, and the judge pauses until Mr Jackson and Mr Evans are standing in front of him.

He continues, "Mr Jackson, are you planning to question your client at this hearing?"

"No, Your Honour," Mr Jackson confirms.

"Mr Evans?"

"No, Your Honour," states Mr Evans.

"Then I would propose that we continue this matter

without the defendant. We cannot make meaningful progress if he is going to keep on interrupting, and I doubt if he will understand much anyway. I see he has started waving to the gallery now. I will not have this behaviour in my court. Any objections?" the judge questions.

Both barristers say no, so Judge Menzies now addresses the official standing beside Aaron in the dock. "I have decided with the agreement of both prosecuting and defence counsels that the defendant does not need to be present at this hearing. Would the officers please return him to the cells."

Once Aaron has been removed, albeit noisily, the judge asks Mr Evans to proceed.

"As I was saying," begins Mr Evans, "the case before us today is a sentencing hearing for Mr Aaron Davis of no fixed abode. At a previous hearing, Mr Davis has admitted to three charges of theft, possession of a knife and the murder of Mr Asif Patel. This was a cruel and totally unnecessary killing of a hard-working and hugely popular community shopkeeper. Mr Patel tried to prevent Mr Davis taking money away from him. Money he had earned working in his shop from 6am that day. Mr Davis went into that shop, not to buy something but to take something. To take Mr Patel's revenue from him. To remove any obstacles in his way in order to find cash to buy drugs. To take Mr Patel's life when he tried to stop the defendant stealing from him. Mr Davis took a knife into the shop with him and he used it to take Mr Patel's life."

At this point, Mr Evans has to stop as loud sobs are heard from the public gallery. Mrs Patel rises and leaves the court, followed by her daughter, both of them crying.

"It should be clear to everyone in this courtroom today that Mr Patel's death has caused massive pain and grief, not only to his family but also to the community. Mr Patel was a pillar of his community and had a reputation for helping anyone in need. Mrs Patel has told me that her husband had given food and money to Aaron Davis in the past, but he had stopped doing so because the defendant sold any items given to him and spent any cash on drugs and alcohol." Mr Evans pauses briefly at this point before continuing. "There is no question that Mr Davis committed this crime. He was identified by two witnesses who know him, and several others described Mr Davis in accurate detail. Mr Davis has, of course, pleaded guilty to these offences. Whilst on remand, the defendant has been medically assessed by a number of expert physicians. The prosecution's view is that Mr Davis clearly has significant reduction in his mental capacity due to the brain damage sustained at his birth. However, his condition has been stabilised in a secure psychiatric unit, mainly through drug therapy. These drugs had been prescribed to Mr Davis on many occasions over the years, but at the time of the offence, he had stopped taking them in favour of cocaine and cheap cider. I would suggest that if Mr Davis had followed his doctor's orders, Mr Patel would still be alive today. The defendant's mental problems are a factor in his behaviour, but the reports show he does know right from wrong, and the majority view contained in the reports is that Mr Davis lashed out through temper, his need for money and his desperation for his next fix. This was a cold-blooded murder carried out by a cold-blooded murderer. The present government, through the Justice Act 2029, has legislated that all convicted murderers must be sentenced to death. In this legislation there exists a procedure set out to deal with defendants who are found by experts to lack mental capacity. Even if the prosecution felt Mr Davis' brain injury and mental state were the reason for his actions, it would still need the agreement of the trial judge, the Court of Appeal and the home secretary to waive the death sentence. As I have already stated the prosecution's view is that the defendant knew right from wrong and proceeded to kill Mr Patel anyway. I ask you, Your Honour, to pass a sentence of death by firing squad on the defendant as the law requires. The prosecution rests, Your Honour."

"Mr Jackson, I imagine you have a fair number of points to make on behalf of the defence?" Judge Menzies enquires.

"Yes, I do, Your Honour," Mr Jackson says as he rises. "Aaron Davis has lived a life that few of us in this courtroom today can imagine. His childhood was spent being left alone for days on end by his mother, followed by living in different foster homes and institutions, which changed every few weeks or months. At eighteen years old, he was removed from his foster home without notice and simply dumped on the street with a few clothes, ten days' supply of medicine and, apparently, a kitchen knife he borrowed from the foster home. Today, you have all seen the state of confusion the defendant is experiencing. That was not a show to impress us. It was how the defendant lives his life – day in, day out. Whilst on the streets, his only relief was cocaine. A bad choice but an inevitable one if you face the life the defendant was living at the time of the crime. Cocaine takes over people's lives. They live only for the next fix. They will do anything to get that next fix. On that fateful day, Aaron Davis needed cocaine. He did not have the money to pay for it, and his dealer wanted hard cash before handing over the drug. Aaron had only one thought in his addled, damaged mind when he went into that shop. That was to get money for cocaine, and nothing and nobody would stop him. Does that sound like cold-blooded murder or the desperate act of a brain-damaged addict? Mr Evans stated that the defendant had admitted to the charges facing him. In fact, Your Honour, Mr Davis did not reply when formally asked for a plea. You then asked him three questions and received three answers, which the court has chosen to accept as guilty pleas. We have all seen today that Mr Davis does not understand simple questions. I would ask you, Your Honour, to agree to a new trial due to the uncertainty about Aaron's ability to understand even simple questions and to answer truthfully."

"That's enough," barks Judge Menzies. "Both counsels to my chambers *now*."

*

The judge's mood has not improved by the time Mr Evans and Mr Jackson are seated in front of him in his chambers.

"Mr Jackson, I will not stand for being criticised in open court for decisions I have already ruled on," remonstrates the judge. "I considered that the defendant understood what I was asking, and he answered sufficiently for me to judge that he was pleading guilty. He was identified, he was caught with the knife and he was holding the money. If you think I am going to order a new trial because he didn't use the word 'guilty', then you are as half-witted as your client. I want an apology, or I will seriously consider contempt charges."

"I apologise, Your Honour," says Mr Jackson through ever so slightly clenched teeth.

"What other points do you intend to make in the remainder of your address? If I know beforehand, perhaps I can avoid sending you to prison."

"I intend to put forward my interpretation of the expert reports and use that to argue that my client needs professional help to improve his life rather than having it ended abruptly."

"That is acceptable, but you know you are completely wasting your time. The Justice Act 2029 states that all convicted murderers are to be sentenced to death. The only provision is if both counsels, the trial judge, the Court of Appeal and the home secretary all agree that a different punishment is appropriate. Mr Evans has already mentioned this in his address to the court. The prosecution have asked for the death sentence, so I cannot see that they are going to support a different type of sentence. I will tell you right now that I feel very strongly that the appropriate sentence here is the death penalty. You can have your say if you like, but you won't change my mind. Therefore, both the prosecution and the trial judge do not want to consider alternative sentencing, and your client's right to claim different punishment is lost. I would strongly suggest, Mr Jackson, that when we return to court, you conclude your address, and we move straight on to sentencing. In absentia, I think. I do not want another set of interruptions from the defendant. Mr Jackson, I will leave it to you and the fragrant Ms Hodgson to pass on the bad news. I'm sure you can make him understand somehow."

*

A few minutes later, Judge Menzies re-enters the court as Mr Jackson and Ms Hodgson confer in whispers at the back of the room.

"Mr Jackson, are you ready to resume your address?" the judge enquires.

"Yes, Your Honour," Mr Jackson says as he walks back into position.

Ms Hodgson bows and leaves the court.

"Your Honour, I do not wish to add anything further," concludes Mr Jackson.

"Excellent. We will move on to the sentencing process. May I ask where Ms Hodgson has gone?" asks Judge Menzies.

"She has gone down to the cells to explain to Mr Davis what is happening."

"Mmm. I miss her delicacy in the court, but I'm sure we'll manage to survive on this occasion. I have decided, after consultation with both counsels, that I will pass the sentence in absentia. That is, I will pass sentence without the defendant being present. It appears our loss is Mr Davis' gain, as he will hear the decision from Ms Hodgson. The Justice Act 2029 states that all murderers will be sentenced to death. There are provisions for variation of the sentence, but as I have already explained to the defence counsel, they do not apply in this case as the criteria for such a manoeuvre are not applicable here. Accordingly, I find that Mr Aaron Davis of no fixed abode is lawfully convicted – on his own pleas – of the murder of Mr Asif Patel, theft and possession of a kitchen knife. I sentence Mr Aaron Davis to death in the manner specified in the Justice Act 2029, at a time and place to be decided by the relevant authority. Any questions, counsellors?"

Mr Jackson rises. "Your Honour, I wish to give

immediate notice of appeal against both conviction and sentence."

"Noted. A complete waste of time and money."

"I would also like to ask that my client be held at his current place of residence in a psychiatric unit rather than being transferred to prison."

"Any objections, Mr Evans?"

"Yes, I have, Your Honour. The medical view is that Mr Davis' problems are controlled if he takes regular medicine. That can be achieved in prison just as easily as in a secure facility. The costs of keeping Mr Davis in custody will be drastically reduced if he is removed to prison," explains Mr Evans.

Mr Jackson stands once more. "Your Honour, my client is a cocaine addict. If he is sent to prison, he will find a way to obtain cocaine, and his condition will deteriorate again very rapidly."

"I see no major problem in holding the defendant in prison. He can be held in the medical ward and monitored as necessary. In the unlikely event that he obtains illicit drugs, I can't really see it will make much difference. After all, he does not have long to live. Aaron Davis is remanded in prison, pending the result of his appeal or the execution of his sentence. It looks like you are passing on that news, Mr Jackson." Judge Menzies picks up his gavel, hits the desk with it and declares, "Case closed."

*

Aaron's appeal is heard in early April 2031, but the appeal judges back the original verdict.

However, by that time, a considerable level of opposition has arisen, led by several newspapers and David McDougall. On 5 May 2031, David appears live on Sara Molan's show to discuss Aaron Davis' case.

"Hello David. Good to see you again. How is life as an independent MP?" enquires Sara.

"Hello Sara and hello to all the viewers. Life is very good now I don't have to obey the pronouncements from above. However, this government juggernaut continues to flatten people in its path and carries on regardless," he states.

"We've asked you in today to talk to us about the case of Aaron Davis, who suffered brain damage at birth and has been sentenced to death for murder. You are leading the campaign to save Aaron's life, which is very commendable, but are you not being a hypocrite when you led Common Sense's law and order campaign at the last general election?"

"No, I don't think that it is at all hypocritical to try to right a terrible injustice. You are right that I campaigned for capital punishment for murderers and tougher sentences for all criminals. I did not write the Justice Act. It was certainly not my intention that anyone should be put to death by the state in such a barbaric manner as being shot down in cold blood by a military firing squad. The additional problem is that Aaron's mental health issues clearly played a part in his actions.

It is not unusual for medical experts to disagree, and unfortunately, the medical assessment reports varied considerably about his awareness of what he was doing."

"There is a set procedure included in the Justice Act that allows an alternative sentence to be utilised in defined circumstances. That clause was, I believe, mentioned by you during the general election, and despite your absence, it has been included in the legislation. The problem is that Aaron Davis does not meet the criteria for being spared the death sentence. There is nothing in the act saying you can be spared if you are a junkie or if you are white or if your victim is not white."

"Sara, come on. That was a low blow even for you. I am not racist and the opposition to this sentence is not based on racism in any way whatsoever."

"Would you still be here if Aaron were black and the victim were white?"

"Yes, of course I would. I worked with you for two years. You know I have never been racist. I denounce racism totally. This campaign is about saving a life. It is about the inflexibility of a brutal government that is determined to put all murderers to death regardless of the circumstances. It is about showing compassion and mercy to someone whom we all abandoned for nineteen years. All those supporting this campaign want to prevent a brutal sentence being inflicted on a confused, scared teenager."

"But what about the victim's family? You told the entire country during the last general election that all murderers would be executed. How do you explain to Mrs Patel and her family that this should not apply to her husband's killer because of his health? If Aaron Davis is treated differently to everyone else, surely it will appear that Mr Patel's life was not as valuable as everybody else's. Is that because he was Indian?"

"No, it is not, and you know that I am not racist in any way. What happened was terrible, and my heart bleeds for the Patel family, who have lost a loved one in dreadful circumstances. Nothing will bring him back, but—"

Sara interrupts at this point. "But surely seeing his killer executed as you promised will at least let them think that Mr Patel's death is being treated in exactly the same way as other murder victims? Every murderer convicted during this government's tenure has been put to death. The Patels are bound to think they are being treated differently if Mr Patel's murderer is allowed to live."

David McDougall is clearly riled by Sara's comments. "I am deeply disappointed by the way you are trying to turn this into a matter of race. It is not a question about the victim now. It is about justice and leniency for a very troubled young man who can be helped and treated with the right medical care. I promise you that I would be taking exactly the same stance if the victim were white, yellow or any other colour you care to mention."

"But what can you do exactly? All appeals have been turned down. The law is clear, and you have admitted this case does not fit the criteria for leniency as laid down in legislation that you helped to create. Are you just trying to gain political points?"

"I am trying to help somebody who cannot help himself."

"Then go and help the Patels."

David McDougall's face turns red as he rises from his chair, rips off his microphone and starts to walk away from the filming area. "I will not stay here to be accused of racism. This is appalling. I will not be treated like this."

Sara carries on calmly and professionally until the end of the programme. However, once she is safely in her dressing room afterwards, she picks up her mobile phone and searches under B in her directory. She makes a call and speaks as soon as the phone is answered. "Hi, it's me. Was that what you wanted? Good, you know I always want to make you happy. By the way, thank you for the lovely flowers. I want red roses next time, after that performance. Bye, darling."

*

Mr McDougall's campaign falters badly after his clash with Sara Molan.

On Monday, 19th May 2031, Aaron Davis is woken at 6.30am, so the execution can be shown live on breakfast TV. He is told by the senior prison officer to take off his pyjamas. Confused and frightened, Aaron refuses and is immediately held tight by two officers whilst two others strip him naked.

Crying and struggling, Aaron is taken out to the prison courtyard and tied to an upright wooden pole. The prison officers move away, and eight soldiers – each carrying an automatic weapon – line up facing the hysterical prisoner. Screams ring out across the courtyard, followed quickly by salvos of automatic fire.

Everything is quiet until military commands ring out, and the soldiers march off, their duty completed.

*

No one comes forward to claim Aaron's body, and he is cremated in a pauper's ceremony with only the priest and undertaker present.

GOVERNMENT PRONOUNCEMENTS

January 2031: Crime is down 43%.
May 2031: Delegating punishment to schools has proved to be a major success in ensuring all misdemeanours are dealt with quickly and at the scene of the crime. This also enables the courts to concentrate on publicly committed serious offences. The Government has now decided to extend this scheme to all employers with immediate effect. Employers will have the legal authority to utilise corporal punishment on employees found guilty of

any crime committed within the workplace. There will be no minimum or maximum restrictions. It is up to individual employers to decide on the appropriate type and scale of the punishment.

CHAPTER 6

MUHAMMED

JUNE 2031 – NOVEMBER 2031

In June 2031, Muhammed Petma's life is as busy and time-restricted as it has been ever since his eldest child started school. His job as a travelling sales representative takes up too many hours each day. Whilst he adores his wife – Fatima – and his two school-age children, he often wishes for a quieter, stress-free existence. Especially on school mornings. Friday, 6th June proves no exception. The kitchen is full of noise, shouts of "*You should have left five minutes ago,*" and childish antics. It is certainly true that Muhammed is already late, and he still has to drop the children at their school.

Finally, the shouting and shooing works, and Muhammed is able to deliver his two children to school. Unfortunately, every other parent seems to be running late as well, and there is nowhere for him to park. Muhammed leaves his car on double yellow lines, takes his children into school and carries on with his day. Following the Government's crackdown on illegal parking, local authorities have installed parking cameras at many problem areas. Muhammed is walking his children into the school building and does not see the camera flash, capturing his vehicle registration as evidence of his illegal actions.

*

Two weeks later, Muhammed receives an unwanted letter in the post: a court summons to appear before the local magistrates' court in three weeks' time. He is not unduly concerned, although Fatima is worried.

"Muhammed, they are cracking down on parking. You could go to jail," she says.

"Don't be silly. It's a flaming nuisance, and there'll be a fine to pay, which we could do without. I'll probably get three points on my licence, but that's no problem as I've had a clean licence for years. The kids must get up earlier. I'm not having this happen again," he responds.

"I hope you're right. But why not just send you a bill to pay? Having to attend court doesn't sound good to me."

Muhammed carries on with his daily routine and doesn't even bother to tell his employers about the situation. He just asks for a day's holiday.

*

On the appointed day, he attends the court along with Fatima and is soon in the dock facing three middle-aged magistrates. A court official reads out the charge, and Muhammed pleads guilty. The magistrate sitting in the centre – a thin, dark-haired woman who looks to be about in her mid-fifties and who has a permanently condescending look on her face – asks Muhammed if he knew he was parking illegally.

"Yes, I did, but I was desperate to get my children into school on time," he explains. "The car was parked there for just over a minute. It seemed the right thing to do at the time. I was concerned with my children and their safety."

"And in doing so, you created a risk for all the other children there, didn't you?" the magistrate asks.

"Um, well, I suppose I did, but that was not my intention. I just didn't think. I just needed to get my children in safely and then get on with my work." Muhammed shifts uncomfortably in the dock and feels sweat beginning to form on his forehead.

"I need to consult with my colleagues on this matter. We will retire for a short time."

A court official tells Muhammed to stay seated in the dock. His mind races as the minutes pass by.

Eventually, the three magistrates come back into the court and everyone rises.

An official tells the standing members of the public

in the courtroom to be seated, but tells Muhammed to remain standing in the dock.

The lady in the middle addresses Muhammed: "Mr Petma, you chose to ignore parking restrictions outside a busy school at morning attendance time. There is a reason why parking is limited in certain places. That reason is the safety of everyone present, but in this case, it is primarily for the safety of all the children arriving for the start of the school day. You have admitted you did not consider anyone other than yourself and your own children. That was a serious misjudgement on your part. We have been made aware that you have no previous convictions and a clean driving licence. The bench feels, however, that this matter is far too serious for us to offer leniency because of your previous unblemished record. You are sentenced to a term of imprisonment for no more than twelve months from today's date. We have considered suspending part or all of this sentence, but we feel unable to do so as it is clearly the Government's intention that sentences should act as a deterrent to both the defendant and the wider population. You are also to be banned from driving any motor vehicle for a period not exceeding three years. This ban is to come into force upon the completion of your term of imprisonment. Case closed. All rise."

"*What? Please, I can't go to jail. I've got a job and a family,*" Muhammed shouts at the retreating magistrates, who take no notice at all. He can also hear, but not see, Fatima crying.

*

"Sorry, mate. No visitors and no phone calls until you've been processed at the prison. You have to stay here until all the cases are finished, and we know how many are joining you on today's mystery trip to a prison of our choice. Don't worry, we'll feed you. Most of our guests reckon that's the first part of the punishment." The guard laughs heartily at his own joke.

Muhammed holds his head in his hands and tries to think of a way out of this mess. "I want to appeal," he says.

"Fine. Tell the officers when you arrive at prison. There's nothing we can do here. We don't do appeals."

*

Muhammed is taken to Kingston Prison, about twenty-five miles from his home. In the first week, he only manages to speak to Fatima once, but he does ask her to see a solicitor urgently about an appeal. He also gets one letter, which is from his employers, dismissing him from his job immediately. Muhammed slowly gets used to prison life, and in some ways, he finds the routine and boredom comforting after years of running around in ever-decreasing circles, making snap decisions constantly.

On his fifteenth day in prison, Muhammed is advised that his wife has been granted permission to visit him during the prescribed visiting time of 2.30pm to 3.30pm. At last, he will know what is happening with getting him out of jail. The time passes even more slowly than usual, but at 2.25pm precisely, he is taken from his cell to the prison gymnasium, which has been transformed into a visiting room with several pairs of chairs set out – each pair having one chair either side of a Perspex screen. All of these individual spaces are numbered. Muhammed is taken, presumably randomly, to space number twelve. Soon afterwards, about twenty or so other people enter, including Fatima, who quickly spots him and makes her way to chair twelve on the visitors' side.

"What a journey. It's taken me two hours to get here and it will be another two hours to get back," Fatima says, clearly irritated. "As if that wasn't bad enough, they've searched me twice already here."

"I was hoping you'd bring the kids," Muhammed tells her.

"What, to a place like this? They're upset enough that you're not at home to take them out. Anyway, I couldn't cope with them on that journey."

"How are they?"

"Fine. They moan every day that they have to walk to and from school."

"I always said you should learn to drive."

"That's a man's role. I wouldn't have parked on a double yellow line and ended up in here."

"There's no chance of that. This is a men's prison," Muhammed replies, with slightly more sarcasm than he really intends. "Have you seen a solicitor? What's happening about an appeal?"

"I've seen a solicitor. He says it will cost at least £1,000, and it is highly unlikely that you will succeed. He says you got off quite lightly. He knows of two people who have been fined and flogged as well as going to prison for doing what you did."

"Look, I've got to get out of here. Put the money on your credit card. Sell something."

"Like what? Your firm took the car back. Nobody wants worn out carpets or your second-hand clothes."

"So, put it on the credit card."

"It's up to its limit."

"What? How? The balance has been nil for months since we paid it off. There's far more than £1,000 on that."

Fatima hesitates and then says firmly, "I have been spending money. I discussed something else with that solicitor: I am divorcing you. I am going back to my mother in Pakistan."

"You can't. Fatima, you can't. What about the children? What about me?"

"What about you? What about me? Left high and dry with two children, no money, no support and the neighbours walking across the road to avoid me."

"You've got your friend Yasmin."

"Yasmeen. She went back to Islamabad months ago. I cannot raise the children on my own. I need help and I need money. I can get both in Pakistan, but not here."

"But, Fatima, I've already done over two weeks of my sentence. Twelve months will soon go by. Please, just be patient."

"Patient for what? Patient for another three years until you can drive again. Patient for weeks, months or years until you find a new job. Patient for ten years until the children are old enough to support us. It is over, Muhammed. Over. You know my mother's address." Fatima rises and starts to leave the room without looking back.

Muhammed kicks away the chair and moves to follow her, but he is quickly dragged to the ground by two prison officers. He is then handcuffed to one of the officers before being returned to his cell.

*

Two hours later, an officer attends Muhammed's cell to advise him he has been placed on a disciplinary charge and will be taken before the governor the next day.

*

A further two hours later, another officer checks on Muhammed through the cell peep-hole and then immediately presses the emergency alarm. Muhammed has hanged himself with his bedsheet. Attempts by prison staff and paramedics fail to revive him, and the duty prison doctor declares him dead at the scene.

GOVERNMENT PRONOUNCEMENTS

September 2031: Crime is down 50% since the last general election, but there is no room for complacency.

October 2031: Common Sense MP for Arundel, Mr Aubrey Hatton, is appointed as the first minister for decency. The minister and the new department will be responsible for monitoring, censoring and authorising all TV, print and online advertisements and programmes from 1st November 2031.

CHAPTER 7

SIMON

NOVEMBER 2031 – MAY 2032

As Christmas 2031 approaches, sixteen-year-old Simon Knight from Kidderminster decides to earn some urgently needed money by taking a part-time job at a local restaurant named The White Cottage, which is run by the Morris family. Initially, Simon is only supposed to work there on Saturday and Sunday lunchtimes, but he quickly finds he is constantly having to cover for other waiting staff on weekday evenings, as they seem to be forever unavailable or sick.

Simon only receives minimum wage and his share of the tips jar. Unfairly, in his view, the share of the tips is based on someone's contracted shifts rather than the actual hours worked.

With his schoolwork suffering, his parents unhappy and less money coming in than he hoped, Simon makes a dreadful mistake and starts taking money from the till when no one is looking. At first, he just takes one or two £1 coins every day or so, but by mid-December he is pocketing £20 or £30 a night. A week before Christmas, his luck runs out, and Mr Morris catches him red-handed taking £20 out of the till at the end of the shift.

His boss takes him into the office and demands an explanation. "What the hell is going on, Simon?"

The schoolboy hesitates before speaking. "I'm so sorry. Here's the money. It won't happen again. I promise." He then hands the bank note over to his employer.

"And the rest?"

"I swear this is the only time."

Mr Morris becomes angry and shouts loudly at him, "*Don't take me for a fool. There's been money missing every time you've worked for weeks. You've had over £200 so far.*"

Simon is shaken and can only say, "I'm so sorry. I'll pay you back; I promise."

"Oh, I'll make absolutely sure of that. But first of all, I'm going to call the police."

Simon reacts with genuine fear. "No, please, Mr Morris. No police. My parents will kill me, and I'll be thrown out of school. Please, no. I promise I'll repay you every penny."

Mr Morris thinks for a minute and then asks. "Do you study law at school?"

Simon shakes his head.

"Do you read the papers?"

"Sometimes."

"Our government in London believes in severe punishment, including for thieves. And that is what you are: a snivelling little thief. What are you?"

Turning bright red with embarrassment and growing more frightened by the second, Simon echoes his boss reluctantly: "A snivelling little thief."

"I'm going to give you a choice. I have the right under recent government law to punish you myself. If you don't want me to do that, then I will hand you over to the police and let them deal with you. If you want to keep this between ourselves then this is what will happen. I will cane you here and now on your backside. Fifty strokes. You will repay me in full before the New Year, and you will never set foot in here again. Do you understand?"

Yes, I do. Please, please, don't cane me though. I couldn't bear it."

"Fair enough," says Mr Morris, picking up the phone.

"No. Wait. May I please keep my clothes on? I'm only sixteen."

"If you are old enough to steal, you are old enough to take the punishment. Come on, hurry up. The cane or the police?"

"The cane," Simon says reluctantly.

To Simon's great relief, Mr Morris puts down the phone. His elation does not last long, as the restaurant owner unlocks a cupboard on the right-hand side of the office and pulls out a thin, crook-handled cane. He swishes it through the air and shivers run down Simon's spine. "Take off your shoes and trousers."

Simon just freezes and looks at him through tear-filled eyes.

"I'm going to count to ten. If you are not undressing by then, I am going to ring the police. This is your last chance to avoid appearing in court and getting much worse than this. One… two… three…"

The teenager sighs deeply and sits down on the chair before removing his left shoe, followed by his right. He then pulls down his trousers. Mr Morris tells him to put them on the desk, which Simon does. Mr Morris comes around the desk and pulls a chair out into the empty space in the middle of the room.

"Kneel on the chair and bend over the back of it," Mr Morris commands.

Simon does what he is told. He can no longer see his boss, but he can hear him swishing the cane. Simon feels it touch his bottom gently and then move away before landing across his underpants with a dreadful hissing sound. The pain comes a few seconds later, and his scream comes shortly after that. Through his pain he can hear Mr Morris call out, "One…"

By the tenth stroke, Simon is screaming all the time, not just when the next stroke lands. By the twenty-fifth, he is begging for mercy. By the fortieth, his entire buttocks feel as though they are on fire, and he is certain he must be raw and bleeding. When the fiftieth stroke comes, he cannot believe he has got through the appalling ordeal.

"That's that," says Mr Morris. "I reckon it will be several days before you sit or sleep properly, though. Stand up and get dressed."

As Simon gets painfully off the chair, Mr Morris turns away from him to put the cane back in the cupboard. He remains with his back to the boy until he is decent again. Simon's trousers are back on, but he is struggling to put his shoes back on without sitting down.

"Now you are sacked for stealing, and I want my money back before the New Year. If you do that, then I will forget all about it, and you can carry on with your education as if nothing has happened," confirms Mr Morris.

Simon hobbles out into the fresh air and immediately rubs his throbbing backside with both hands. He collects his bicycle, but he knows there is no chance at all of riding it. Instead, he has no choice but to limp home pushing the bike, thinking the whole way how he is going to explain his tear-stained face, his throbbing bottom and his new found unemployment to his parents.

He is forced to walk slowly as every step reawakens the pain in his posterior. Eventually, he arrives home and very reluctantly goes inside.

"Whatever has happened to you? You look terrible and you've been crying!" Simon's mother exclaims, rising from her chair.

However, this natural sympathy does not last long, as Simon tells his parents the events of that evening.

"I am ashamed of you," snaps his mother when Simon has finished. "Stealing from Mr Morris. I never thought you were capable of something like that. Get to bed. We will talk about this tomorrow."

*

The next day, Simon's parents ground him for a month, make him write an apology to Mr Morris (including thanking him for the punishment) and make it clear that he must repay the money himself with no help from them. Simon sells his bicycle and returns the money to Mr Morris in full before the deadline.

*

William Marshall, head of current affairs, rarely visits the studios, but he has made an exception in order to talk to Sara Molan in her dressing room about an hour before her show starts. "Sara, you are going to have to raise your game. The BBC are starting a new show next month to clash with your programme. They have signed up Sue Horton to present it."

"What do I have to worry about? She'll only attract the grandma viewer. God, she must be at least fifty," scoffs Sara.

"Well, that's as may be, but she has a reputation for being an easy interviewer. We are not going to find it easy to get the big players on here for you to chew up and spit out when they can get an easy ride over there."

"People want to see politicians sweat and actually answer the questions. They will soon be bored with sweet Sue handing out cups of tea and asking her guest what their favourite sandwich is."

"Look, Sara, I want higher ratings. You may be right in the long term, but this will hit us badly. David McDougall has not returned my calls since you mauled him, and there are plenty of others avoiding ten rounds with you. I want that exclusive interview you keep promising with Godwin, and I want it now."

Mr Marshall departs, leaving Sara to her thoughts. She looks at the flowers in the corner of the room and says a silent prayer of thanks that she had removed the card from them before her big boss arrived. She retrieves the card from her make-up drawer and reads the latest message from the prime minister: "These flowers are the most beautiful in London, but you make them look like weeds. Love, Bob."

Sara thinks, *I hope you mean that. It's time to stop playing.*

Sara dials the first number in her phone's memory. When it has connected, it goes straight to voicemail: "This is my private number. Unless I have given you this number personally, hang up. Otherwise, leave a message now."

"Bob, hi. Thank you for the flowers. We need to talk urgently. I'm close to programme time now, but please ring me this afternoon or evening. Love you. Bye," she says.

GOVERNMENT PRONOUNCEMENTS

January 2032: Crime is down 52%, but there has been a significant rise in the number of sex offences coming before the courts. Adultery convictions have risen by 33% during the last twelve months. Punishments for adultery will be increased with immediate effect, in order to reverse this worrying upsurge in offences. All convicted adulterers will be jailed for a minimum of twelve years, and will receive a minimum total of 1,000 strokes of the cane and a minimum total of 1,000 strokes of the nine-tailed whip. All convicted adulterers will be branded.

March 2032: All convicted sex offenders must be sentenced to at least 1,000 strokes in total of the nine-tailed whip.

CHAPTER 8

WARREN

MAY 2032 – NOVEMBER 2032

Warren was born in August 2022, and is nine years old at the present time. Even though he has attended school for nearly five years, the basic requirements of sitting still, listening to the teacher and learning mean nothing at all to him. His reports regularly use words such as "naughty", "disruptive" and "rude". The school punishment book contains Warren's name more than any other pupil. In April 2032, he received thirty-six strokes of the cane on his bare bottom for using the F word during an argument with his class teacher. He has not learned his lesson at all and continues to wreak havoc in the classroom every day.

As usual, Warren is running around the room during an art lesson. He stops at the back of the room by Lauren's desk. Lauren is also nine years old, with an angelic face and beautiful blonde curls. She also happens to be the quietest, shyest girl in the class and the principal's granddaughter.

"Do you want to see my willy?" Warren asks her.

Lauren concentrates on her painting, and Warren soon finds someone else to torment, before actually sitting down at his own desk for a few minutes. This does not last very long, and like a homing pigeon, he heads straight back to Lauren.

This time, he decides actions speak louder than words, and after moving as close to his victim as possible, he pulls down his trousers and pants, then says, "There it is. You can touch it if you like."

Lauren bursts into tears and runs out of the classroom. The rest of the class laugh, shout and cheer. Warren just stands there, with his trousers and pants around his ankles and a wicked grin all over his face. The art teacher, Miss Grant, has barely started to restore order when the principal, Mr Graves, enters the room.

"*Silence!*" he roars. "*Everyone sit down now.*"

Warren decides the easiest thing to do is sit down at Lauren's desk, since he's already there.

Mr Graves continues, "Miss Grant, outside please. The rest of you stay where you are, and if I hear one word from anyone, you will all be caned."

Even Warren gets the message that Mr Graves is in no mood to be challenged, and he sits there quietly improving Lauren's painting.

*

Outside in the corridor, an animated conversation is taking place.

"Whatever has happened in there, Miss Grant? Lauren has burst into my office crying her eyes out, saying Warren wants her to touch his willy," queries Mr Graves.

"Well, I was helping Andrew, who had spilled paint over himself. A minute earlier, Warren had been sitting at his own desk. When I heard Lauren burst into tears and rush outside, I looked in the direction of her desk and Warren was standing there with his trousers and underpants around his ankles. Principal, we have got to do something about him once and for all. He needs to be in a bad-behaviour class or taught one on one. I've got twenty-nine other children in there. I cannot watch him every second," declares Miss Grant.

"No, I understand. I am not blaming you, at all. I can cane him again and try to make him understand he cannot behave like this. He will cry again and say he does not want to be caned again. Five minutes later, he will be all smiles and misbehaving as badly as ever."

"What about his parents, Principal? Are they any help?"

"None whatsoever. They say he is a saint at home. He never causes them any trouble. They have tried to stop us disciplining him at all, but this government fortunately insists all children can and must be beaten when appropriate. By heavens, it is appropriate right now." Mr Graves looks into the classroom, where Warren is sitting with a butter-wouldn't-melt expression on his face, working hard at Lauren's artwork. "I left Lauren with my secretary, so I will go back to the office and persuade her to come back to class. Get Warren dressed again and make him stand in the corner with his face to the wall. I will speak to his mother and then come back to collect him."

*

Lauren duly returns to the classroom and, after checking that Warren is both fully dressed and nowhere near her desk, returns to her rightful place. It only takes two seconds for her to let out a loud scream and run out of the room again in the general direction of her grandad's office. Miss Grant goes to Lauren's desk to see what the problem is this time, only to discover that the girl's simple-yet-evocative picture of a house and garden has been obliterated by Warren's favourite four letter word in just about every colour it is possible to create from half a dozen paints. The teacher tries hard not to laugh. Warren is grinning like a Cheshire cat, but nobody can see him.

*

Meanwhile, Mr Graves has problems of his own as he is speaking to Warren's mother on the phone: "I understand your position, but I do not need your permission to cane your son. His behaviour today is totally unacceptable. I shall be talking to the education department at county hall about alternative education arrangements for Warren. I want you to keep him home for the time being. I do not want him here until the experts have decided how best to educate him without ruining school life for everyone else in the form. Hello… Hello… Blast it, she has hung up on me. Dreadful woman."

After finishing speaking to Warren's mother and – latterly – himself, Mr Graves pulls the punishment book down from its shelf. He writes the date and the pupil's name in the relevant columns, and then muses over how to complete the remainder of the entry.

When he has finished, he phones his secretary and says, "Would you find Warren's class teacher, Miss Johnson, and get her to come to my office right away? If she is teaching, you will have to stay with her class whilst she's away, I am afraid. This could take a while."

A few minutes later, there is a knock on Mr Graves' office door.

"Come in," he says.

Miss Johnson enters. "What on earth has he done this time?"

"Exposed himself to my granddaughter and then written the F word all over her picture. I have needed to get her mother in to take her home."

"How many are you going to give him this time?"

Mr Graves pushes the punishment book across to Miss Johnson.

She looks at the entry. "Are you sure? Have you told the parents?"

"I have spoken to his mother. She insists we need her permission, but we do not, of course. I have told her to come and collect Warren at the usual time. Our nurse will no doubt need to have a good look at him after I've finished with his backside."

"How do you intend to do this? We had enough trouble giving him thirty-six last time."

"I honestly think the best way is for you to sit on a chair, put him across your lap and hold on to him as tightly as possible. Otherwise, he is just going to be running around the room with us trying to catch him like last time. Are you happy to do that?"

"Of course, Mr Graves."

"Right, I will go and get him."

The principal walks back to Warren's classroom and marches the boy back to the office in silence. Once inside, Mr Graves tells Warren to undress.

"Wish you'd make your minds up," Warren mutters disgruntledly. "Put them on, stand there, come here, take them off."

"Not one more word out of you," states Mr Graves. "You are in more than enough trouble for one day. Do you understand why?"

"Yes. I upset Lauren. She's not my friend any more. She's a telltale."

Miss Johnson manages to speak before the principal. "Come on, Warren. More undressing and less conversation."

The boy takes off his shoes and trousers, and then looks hopefully at Miss Johnson. It is to no avail.

"And the rest."

With a sigh, Warren removes his T-shirt, vest and socks before another hopeful glance in his teacher's direction.

This time, Mr Graves' voice responds. "Get your pants off now, boy, or I will double your punishment."

Even Warren knows when to give in gracefully, and his underpants immediately join the higgledy-piggledy pile of clothes on the floor. It is left to Miss Johnson to fold the clothing and place it on a chair. She then pulls another chair into the middle of the room, sits down and tells Warren to join her. She then grabs him and pulls him full length across her lap before grabbing him tightly around his waist. "Is that all right for you?"

The question is meant for Mr Graves, but the culprit answers first: "No. I'm uncomfortable and cold."

"Part of you will be very hot soon," retorts Mr Graves. "Yes, Miss Johnson, that will be fine as long as you can hold him tight." He turns and unlocks a cupboard before selecting a thick, yellowish cane.

"Now, Warren, this is going to hurt a lot. This is a heavier cane than I have used on you before, and you are going to get 100 strokes. The most you have had before is thirty-six. Now keep still, and it will be over much more quickly. I will count the strokes, Miss Johnson. You concentrate on keeping him straight and on your lap."

Warren seems disinterested, but not for long. The first stroke soon lands across the boy's bare bottom, and a thick, red line appears instantaneously across his white skin. Warren yells and starts to cry.

"One." The principal waits a few seconds and then repeats the action with the same results. "Two."

The thrashing continues, but after fifty strokes, Miss Johnson insists that they have a break. She doesn't let go of the screaming Warren, though. "Mr Graves, I think we need to get the nurse to look at him. His bottom is red hot and must be dreadfully sore. I think you are going to break the skin and make him bleed if you carry on."

"That is exactly what I intend to do. He is fine at the moment. Let us carry on. We're halfway. Fifty-one next."

Warren is far too distressed to be interested. All too soon from his point of view, the vicious strokes start landing again.

Finally, the punishment is complete.

"One hundred. Hold on to him for a minute. I will get the nurse now," says the principal as he opens the door and goes out.

He soon returns with the school nurse.

"Just what have you done to this poor boy's bottom?" the nurse exclaims. "Blimey, I have never seen a caning that severe." She grabs hold of Warren, as Miss Johnson releases him, and puts him down gently on the floor. "Stay there a minute, dear. I'll just get a blanket. You won't be able to stand having your clothes on and it wouldn't be right to walk you through the school naked." With that, she leaves in search of a blanket.

Warren continues to cry out in agony.

Mr Graves bends down to the boy's height and declares, "I hope you learn your lesson well and that this is the first and last time anyone has to punish you as severely as this."

The nurse soon returns, enfolds Warren in the blanket and gathers up his clothes. She then helps the boy walk to her medical room.

Miss Johnson shakes some life into her arms. "That is the worst thing I have experienced in all my years teaching. Are you sure he needed that many to get the message across?"

"Thirty-six meant nothing to him. As soon as he stops crying, he forgets all about it. He will remember this for a long time."

"So will his parents, I fear," sighs Miss Johnson.

GOVERNMENT PRONOUNCEMENTS

May 2032: Crime is down 55% since the last general election. A massive US trade deal is now signed. Currently, the economy is underperforming. Tax rises are being considered. With immediate effect, the

Government – acting on advice from nutrition experts – advises every citizen to eat red meat at least twice a week. The Government will shortly introduce legislation to make vegetarianism and veganism illegal.

*

Sara Molan is having a bad week. William Marshall is unhappy about the ratings being attained by Sue Horton's rival programme and is demanding Sara delivers the promised interview with the prime minister sooner rather than later. Bob Godwin, of course, isn't returning her calls, although she has three vases full of new flowers from him. On top of all this, she is about to watch her rival's show from earlier in the day. She knows it will not be pleasant viewing as Sue's guest is David McDougall, who is publicising his latest campaign against the Government.

Sara settles down in her chair and listens to the theme music.

"Hello and welcome to today's edition of *The Sue Horton Show*. My guest is the doyen of TV presenters, turned independent MP, Mr David McDougall. Hello David, and thank you for agreeing to be on the programme," welcomes Sue.

"Thank you for inviting me, Sue. It is always a pleasure to work with you," David replies with a smile.

"Smarmy git," snaps Sara, as she reaches for a chocolate – courtesy of the prime minister, of course.

"Now, David," Sue continues on the TV, "you are

here today to talk about a campaign you have started to force the Government to deal with something that you and many others see as a major injustice. Would you like to tell us about this?"

"Willingly. Everyone in this country is now under the constant threat of being dragged into the merciless jaws of this dreadful government's justice system. But I am particularly concerned about some of the most vulnerable in our society, namely the very young. 'Beating' Bob Godwin and his far-from-merry gang have seen fit to remove the age limit for criminal responsibility. Previously, this ensured that children under the age of ten could not be prosecuted or punished for their so-called 'crimes'. Now they are considered fair game, along with the rest of us. This age limit was introduced not out of kindness but because young children do not have the same awareness of right and wrong as us oldies do. This has concerned me for some time, but the case of Warren is so awful that it is time for sensible people to act."

"Not all our viewers may be aware of the situation with Warren. Perhaps you could tell us a bit more about it?"

"Warren is nine years old. He is a bit naughty at school, as many boys that age are. He has regularly been caned over the last two years with no improvement in his behaviour. So, he keeps on getting caned more and more severely. His parents do not believe in discipline and have not given permission for Warren to be beaten.

That means nothing to this government. They say that any child in school can be physically punished whether the parents want that to happen or not. In theory, a four-year-old can be beaten brutally and no one can stop it. A few days ago, Warren was made to strip naked in the presence of the male principal and a female teacher. He was then caned – not with six of the best or even twelve of the best but an unbelievable 100 times with a senior cane, which should not be used on children under eleven."

Sara, at home, shouts at the TV, "*Tell us what he did. Tell us.*"

David continues. "This is brutality at its worst. And the fault lies with Bob Godwin. He has introduced the law of the savage to this great country, and it is time that the ordinary, kind-hearted majority rise up to stop this carnage. Warren cannot sit, he cannot lie on his back and he cannot even put on clothes. His mother took him home from that school of torture covered only by a blanket. Sue, this has to be stopped before a young child is maimed for life. There is no limit to the punishment that can be inflicted. Older children regularly receive floggings into the hundreds or even thousands of lashes. Enough is enough. I am determined to get the age of responsibility reinstated and for parents to regain control over how their children are disciplined."

As Sue prepares to speak in the studio, Sara yells at her, "*For God's sake, Sue, ask him what Warren did.*"

"I agree wholeheartedly with you, David. But what

exactly can you do? You are no longer a member of the ruling party. Do you have any influence at all to stop barbarity like this?" Sue queries.

Sara groans and holds her head in her hands as David starts to speak: "I have some influence in Parliament, and both major opposition parties have joined me in condemning this cruelty. I readily admit, though, that I need help from everyone in this country. Not just those affected by this but everyone who knows in their heart that torturing young children is wrong on every level."

"So, what can I and everybody else do?"

Sue's appeasing words bring forth a volley of abuse from a totally exasperated Sara, but of course no one hears her frustration.

"Sue, I have started a petition," confirms David. "You can find it on my website. I urge everyone to sign this. Please show the Government that there is a line they cannot cross, and we will not sit back for a moment longer and watch children being scarred for life. I want the whole country to rise up – peaceably, of course. Write to your MP. Write to the prime minister. Write to your children's school. The time has come to show Mr Godwin we have had enough of his pronouncements. I am a democrat. This proud nation is a democracy, and we must all act now before there are no freedoms left to fight for. Sue, there are so many injustices happening daily in this country, and yet all the Government can do is persecute vegans. What on earth is all that about? Was the prime minister's mother scared by a cabbage?

The threat from within this country is very real, and we must all take peaceful action now to put an end to this nonsense."

"Thank you so much for that, David. I am going to sign your petition as soon as the programme is over. The website address for David McDougall is on your screens right now. Please support David in this."

Sara turns off the TV with a deep sigh and mutters to herself: "Stupid, bloody woman. Why didn't you just lick his arse for him? Fucking useless amateur." Still cursing to herself, she picks up her phone and presses redial. "Now, you have to speak to me, darling. You have just as many problems as I have. Watch Sue Horton's love-in with McDougall if you don't believe me. If this interview doesn't happen, like, yesterday, you and I will both be looking for new jobs. Ring me."

CHAPTER 9

BOB

EARLY JUNE 2032

Sara Molan is not sleeping well. She still hasn't really got used to sleeping alone. She misses Nic's late night kisses and cuddles. She misses the sex. She hates waking up alone.

That would be enough on its own, but her work problems are keeping her awake at night too. David McDougall has struck a nerve with the British public, and various forms of protest are beginning to gain momentum. Sue Horton's ratings are rising. Hers are falling. Not dramatically, but enough to make her anxious about her future.

These night time worries are the reason she is up working at 5am. For the tenth time since David's triumph on Sue Horton's programme, she rings the prime minister's private mobile, ready to leave another angry, worried message. To her total amazement, the phone is answered on the third ring.

"Hello Sara. What time of day do you call this? Even prime ministers are allowed some sleep," Bob says, surprisingly good naturedly.

"You're damn lucky if you sleep at all. You ought to try sleeping in my bed sometimes. That is not an invitation, by the way. Not yet anyway," she replies.

"Aah, has Sara got some problems? Let Bob sort them out for you, and then we can go back to bed. Separately, of course."

"The only way you can help is by ending your invisible-man impression and doing an interview. With me and nobody else."

"All right. Let's do that then."

"What did you just say?"

"Let's do the interview. Get your producer or one of his flunkies to ring my press secretary. I am a busy man. Could we do the interview in Downing Street?"

"My producer is a woman, and I doubt she knows what a flunky is. The interview will have to be in the studio because we are a live programme."

"All right, I will agree to that but no audience. And I want the full hour's programme to myself. No adverts, no breaks. Just an hour of polite questions and answers."

"No questions to be given in advance, and I can cover any subject at all."

"Agreed, apart from our relationship."

Sara is about to say what relationship, but she decides

not to muddy the waters with the elusive interview finally in her grasp. Instead, she says, "That's fine. I will ring your secretary myself. I'm not taking any chances at all on this."

"Unlike us, she starts at 9am. Bye Sara, pleasant dreams."

The line goes dead. Sara punches the air, shouting, "*Yes!*" several times, far too loudly for the hour.

*

Two weeks later, the tension in the studio is at fever pitch. William Marshall has taken charge personally, and several other senior managers are standing around, making small talk and looking nervous. Sara is in her dressing room, surrounded by flowers and good luck messages, including one from Sue Horton.

There is a knock on the door, and the stage manager enters. "The prime minister is here. We've put him in the green room if you want to see him. It's amazing. He just strolled in here with no entourage at all. Five minutes, and then you need to be in the studio."

She gathers up her notes and glances at them for the twentieth time, before finishing her make-up and checking her appearance in the mirror. "Time to see off stupid Sue once and for all," she murmurs to herself.

Sara makes her way to the green room. Bob Godwin is impeccably dressed in a dark-blue suit. He smiles as Sara enters and walks over to embrace her.

"We need to be in the studio in two minutes and then on air in seven," she says.

"Doing anything tonight?"

"Celebrating or drowning my sorrows. Which one it will be is really in your hands."

"Whichever you are doing, you should not be alone. Give me a ring later if you want to."

Sara nods and tells the prime minister that the time has come to head for the studio. On the way, Bob holds her hand briefly before Sara pulls away, saying. "Not here. Perhaps later."

"Just be gentle with me," Bob replies. "Now and later."

They quickly arrive at the studio. Mr Marshall introduces himself to the prime minister, and they all make their way to the set.

"Thirty seconds to theme music," Sara hears in her right ear. She repeats the message to Bob and reaches across the desk to touch his hand. "I'll be gentle with you," she says.

"Theme music started," confirms the voice in Sara's ear. "Fifteen seconds to air. Ten. Five… four… three… two… one. On air, Sara."

She begins, "Hello, I'm Sara Molan, and today, the entire programme will be devoted to an exclusive interview with the prime minister, Bob Godwin. Welcome, Prime Minister."

"Hello Sara and hello to all the great citizens of this country who are watching," Bob replies.

"To start with, Prime Minister, this is your first interview since your interview with me immediately after the last general election. Do you think it has been wise to hide yourself away from the people you serve?"

"I believe that I owe it to the country to do as good a job as I can. Being prime minister is a huge honour, and one I take very seriously. It is close to being a twenty-four-hour-a-day job. I made the decision that I could be of more service in this role if I concentrated on the work and the decisions, and left communication to others. I believe that the public has been kept up to date on important government decisions. To me, it does not matter who delivers the news as long as it is delivered. I may have been out of sight, but I can assure you that I have been working day and night to ensure our manifesto promises are kept. Crime is down over 50%. The economy is struggling at the moment, mainly because of the ridiculous terms of the Brexit treaty negotiated by my predecessor. I have now cancelled that treaty and it has been replaced very recently by a magnificent trade treaty with the USA. It will take time for us to see the benefits, but they will come."

"You stated in your manifesto that you would not increase taxes, yet there has been a recent pronouncement that you are considering increasing taxes. Surely, this is a case of you blatantly lying to the electorate?"

"As I just said, the economy is struggling temporarily. This is due entirely to switching from a bad trade deal to a good trade deal. I have managed to keep all manifesto promises to date. Circumstances do change from time to time. It would be a huge disappointment to me if taxes did have to be increased. If that does happen – and at present, it is just something being considered – then I can assure the nation that any rises will be small and short term."

"Before we move on to the complicated issues surrounding law and order, I would like to ask you about your decision to ban veganism and vegetarianism. Your government has been accused by David McDougall of entering into people's bedrooms. Now you seem to be taking over their kitchens as well."

"Are you a vegetarian, Sara?"

"Yes, I am, but if you are going to throw me in prison or flog me for not eating meat, then I guess I won't be for much longer."

"I can immediately put your mind at rest about this. Nobody will be hauled before the courts or punished in any way for continuing to have a vegan or vegetarian diet. The worst that will happen is people who do not want to enjoy a more balanced diet will be required to attend a course setting out the disadvantages of vegetarian and vegan lifestyles. If anybody attends the course but still feels that they wish to remain vegetarian or vegan, then that is their free choice to make. This is not a crazy idea or a fad, as some of my critics have suggested. David McDougall even proposed that my mother might have been frightened by a cabbage. My late mother loved cabbage. I do not like cabbage, but I do eat many other vegetables. There have been many reports from reputable organisations throughout the world suggesting that veganism, in particular, does not provide a healthy lifestyle. In the last three months alone, there have been two damning reports issued by well-respected organisations highlighting significant dangers in these diets."

"The pronouncement stated that the Government would be introducing legislation to ban vegetarianism and veganism. Now you are saying that there is no ban, just advice. So, which is right?"

"What I have said today is now government policy. We did think about a total ban, but ultimately, we decided against that. I thought a pronouncement had been issued about this change, but apparently not."

"Perhaps you should rethink your communication system or else be interviewed by me every month or so. Is this a climb down on your part?"

"As I have already said, it is a rethink. If there has been any misunderstanding, then I apologise. I feel I need to repeat that nobody will be prosecuted over this or punished for continuing to eat only items from a vegan or vegetarian lifestyle."

"Prime Minister, many people watching today will feel they have just witnessed a government climbdown on this."

"Then they are wrong. This is a rethink, not a climbdown. This government will continue to do everything possible to enable all citizens to lead as healthy a lifestyle as possible. It is a major priority of mine to reduce obesity and the level of weight-related deaths from diabetes, strokes and heart attacks. I would strongly urge everybody to look carefully at government health advice and take individual responsibility for their weight, diet and lifestyle."

"Now I would like to ask you about your law and order policies. I am sure you are aware that there is currently a considerable amount of upset about the use of corporal punishment on children under the age of ten. That is not the only area of disquiet, but perhaps we could start with that and move on to other areas of concern later?"

"Sara, that is fine with me. I will address the issue you mentioned, but I would like to say first of all that this upset, as you call it, is largely down to the actions of one man: Mr David McDougall, former joint leader of the Common Sense Party and someone I had considered – until I became prime minister – as a good and trusted friend. During his time as joint leader of the party, David was involved in detailed discussions about every item in our manifesto for the last general election. All drafts and the final wording of the manifesto were seen by David, and they contained the promise to get rid of the right of children aged ten years and younger to escape prosecution and punishment for their crimes. I attended many meetings of the executive committee and at no point did David raise any objections to the abolition of the age limit for criminal responsibility. I am disappointed that he is ignoring his own part in manifesto decisions, to criticise a government he has no connection to any longer."

"Prime Minister, may I just interrupt your flow for a minute? I would love to hear your account of how you became prime minister rather than Mr McDougall."

"On general election night, I waited at my London constituency for the votes to be counted. After I had been declared the winner, I drove to party headquarters. The chairman of the executive committee asked to have a private word with me and offered me the post of sole leader of the Common Sense Party. He told me that this decision would also mean that I would be the next prime minister, if the general election predictions of a massive victory proved to be true. I decided to accept the position and the great responsibility that comes with it."

"So, you are saying you had no part to play in removing David from the joint leadership?"

"Yes, I am saying that because it is the truth."

"Do you know why the executive committee made that decision?"

"No, you will have to ask them. I know David feels I betrayed him, but that is simply not the case. Even if it were, it would still be hypocritical of him to lay the blame for abolishing the age of criminal responsibility solely at my door. He endorsed the manifesto and actively campaigned in favour of the entire document."

"Turning now to a case that has attracted much publicity: the painful experience of Warren. A nine-year-old who was given 100 strokes of the cane at school. Many people feel children that young should not be beaten or no child of that age should be punished so severely. Over 3 million residents of this country have now signed David McDougall's petition calling on you to reintroduce an age of criminal responsibility and to reduce massively the maximum number of strokes any school pupil can receive."

"Warren is a disruptive child who has been caned on several occasions, mainly for running wild in the classroom during lessons and for swearing. On the day in question, Warren exposed himself to a female classmate, also nine years old. The girl was so terrified of Warren's behaviour that she fled the classroom in tears and, eventually, had to be collected from school and taken home by her mother. As if that was not enough, Warren also wrote swear words over the girl's artwork. The principal of the school has a legal duty to keep all his pupils safe. He also has a legal obligation to punish naughty children, with no limits on the amount of punishment and without needing parental permission."

"Do you think that last point is fair? Many parents do not want their children beaten, and until 2029, they had the legal right to say no."

"In this case, is it fair that Warren should escape meaningful punishment? He has been made to stand in the corner, but he giggles throughout. He has been given detentions, but his parents insist they can only collect him at the normal leaving time, so he never attends detention. He has been given lines, but again, his parents will not agree to let him do them. Whilst children are in school, the local authority and, ultimately, the Government are responsible for the safety of all pupils. I welcome parental responsibility, and in this case, some degree of cooperation from the family might have improved the situation. Personally, I feel that this is exactly the kind of situation where it is right that the school principal can make unilateral decisions to inflict punishment and preserve the safety of every other pupil."

"Three million people feel differently."

"Please do not forget that over 30 million people voted for the Common Sense Party at the last general election. They voted for a clampdown on crime. They voted for the reintroduction of the death penalty for all murderers. They voted for the return of the cane to schools. My duty lies with those voters. My job is to ensure that their wishes are carried out during my tenure as prime minister. I understand people's concerns about this case. Perhaps if Warren's parents spent less time complaining and more time teaching their son the right way to behave, we would not need to have this debate at all."

"That is rather a narrow view, Prime Minister. Schools must have a role to play in educating children in correct behaviour as well as in academic subjects."

"I do agree with you, but the emphasis must be on schools playing a part. Families must be part of the process as well. I also feel that it is right that the school can reinforce its part with meaningful punishment."

"In Warren's case, that just means increasing the number of strokes each time. Thirty-six didn't stop him, so let's try 100. If that doesn't work what comes next, Prime Minister? One hundred and fifty? Two hundred? How about 1,000? All on a nine-year-old boy's bare bottom. We are not in medieval days. Surely you must appreciate that punishments like this are truly repulsive to many people watching this interview."

"Sara, you are getting into the realms of fantasy. Of course, you cannot just keep upping the punishment in cases like this, but thirty-six strokes is not the place to stop. In some cases, 100 would be. In another case, it is worth persevering with more severe punishments to see if the pattern of bad behaviour and punishment can be broken. I was informed by the relevant local authority just before coming to the studio today that they feel Warren is not suited to the conventional learning environment. It has been decided to teach him on a one-to-one basis for at least the next year. If genuine progress is made, then an attempt will be made to reintroduce Warren to multi-pupil teaching once more."

"Presumably, though, he will still be beaten if he misbehaves?"

"Well, hopefully, he will improve when there are no classmates for him to annoy and harass. The truthful answer to your question is that if he continues to misbehave, then he will almost certainly receive further canings. I make no apology for that. Common Sense won a general election with a huge majority, campaigning – amongst other things – for the return of corporal punishment to schools."

"If the petition gets 30 million signatories, will you change the policy?"

"No. People can vote against us at the next general election if they are not happy with the way we have governed in our current five-year term of office."

"Prime Minister, I would like to discuss another school punishment that made the headlines a couple of years ago. A schoolgirl called Leah attacked another pupil and accidentally knocked over a teacher. She received a total of 500 strokes of the cane in less than twenty-four hours. She was naked throughout the punishments, and 300 of the strokes were administered in front of other pupils. I am surprised the beatings weren't filmed and released on S&M [sadism and masochism] sites on the internet. How can you possibly justify that kind of humiliation and pain for a teenage schoolgirl?"

"Again, this was a serious incident in which another pupil was hurt badly enough to require hospital treatment. The circumstances here were quite different to Warren's case. This was a one-off incident involving a dispute about a boy, and Leah's parents were extremely supportive of the punishment. Indeed, I understand that she was beaten at home in addition to the canings at school. The Government has deliberately left the decisions concerning the number of strokes and other details of the punishments to individual head teachers. They know the pupils, the background to the case and exactly what punishment fits the crime. Sara, you must also bear in mind that there are a number of elements to any punishment. One is a deterrent factor, which is extremely important in schools. Seeing someone you spend several hours a day with being beaten is an excellent way to learn not to make the same mistake yourself. Secondly, there is pain. In the case of caning, it is physical pain. In the case of detention or lines, it is a pain of inconvenience of losing your own private time by being forced to do something you do not want to be doing at that time. Thirdly, there is humiliation. I feel punishment is bound to be more effective if it is carried out in front of witnesses or involves the removal of clothing. I quite like your idea of putting film of beatings on the internet. Not school punishments, of course, but it is certainly something to consider that would add to the humiliation for adult prisoners."

"I think we now need to move on to death sentences. In view of what you have just said, perhaps you could tell us whether you are going to invite people along to watch executions. They are already broadcast live. It could make a good family day out with a picnic breakfast and a chance for granny to catch up on her knitting."

"I love it when you become sarcastic. I have no plans to invite guests inside prisons to witness executions. TV stations, such as this one, want ratings and millions of people tune in to see the firing squads in action."

"You are being defiant about your policies today, but many people – including me – feel the death penalty is one step too far. I want to talk about Aaron Davis. His execution continues to concern many people in this country. We were able, if we wished, to see a nineteen-year-old brain-damaged man tied naked to a post and brutally cut down by a military firing squad. This is the twenty-first century, not the Dark Ages. Why on earth do you think making an entertainment spectacular out of death is a good idea?"

"The main point here, which you are missing completely, is that this is not down to me. David McDougall, the executive committee of Common Sense and I drew up a general election manifesto that included bringing back the death penalty for all murderers. Thirty million people supported that policy by voting the party into power."

"Agreed, but the devil is in the detail. Do you still think those people would have supported you if they knew the reality of naked human beings being ripped to pieces by military gunfire live on TV? You can't lay the blame on David for this one. The manifesto gave no details of the process of execution. He was not involved in writing or overseeing the Justice Act 2029, which did contain full details of the execution method. I live in the real world, and I can tell you that the manner in which murderers are murdered themselves by the state distresses many, many residents of this country. There needs to be changes made urgently to your sadistic, medieval policies."

For the first time, Bob Godwin looks taken aback by the ferocity of the host's comments. When he speaks, he is clearly angry and raises his voice as he talks. "Sara, that is your opinion, and it may or may not be shared by others. Thirty million people supported our policies at the last general election. Murder is a terrible act. Aaron Davis stabbed a hard-working shopkeeper to death for a few pounds in order to buy drugs. There are processes in place to ensure truly mentally damaged people – who, in the opinion of experts, genuinely do not understand right from wrong – are not put to death. That was not in the manifesto, although it was mentioned during the general election campaign by David, me and several other parliamentary candidates. It is an essential safeguard, which I insisted upon. In this case, the majority opinion of medical professionals, not TV presenters or the general public, found that Mr Davis did not meet the criteria to be punished in a different way. All methods of execution are horrible. Hanging can go wrong; for instance, Babbacombe Lee, the man they couldn't hang. Lethal injection can sometimes take many minutes to work. The guillotine would work, but nowadays, there would definitely be a backlash about severed heads rolling into baskets. There is no kind way to carry out a death sentence, despite what you, David McDougall and Sue Horton might think. I am not a sadistic murderer. I am a dedicated prime minister who is trying to fulfil his party's general election promises. Scum like Aaron Davis cannot be left to roam our streets, killing indiscriminately. Crime is down over 50% overall. Murders are down 70% since 2029. My methods are working. The streets are safer. If a few criminals die horribly or a few schoolchildren end up with sore bottoms, then so be it. Where crime is concerned, the ends justify the means. I have no sympathy for any criminal, but murderers are the lowest of the low. They are vermin, and no punishment or degradation is too much for any of them. I shall never worry about a murderer being shot or a child being caned. They deserve everything they get, and anyone who supports them – or signs petitions to prevent criminals being adequately punished – is a traitor to this country and all law-abiding, right-minded citizens."

"Prime Minister, do you consider that I am a traitor to my adopted country just because I found Aaron Davis' public execution to be horrific and unnecessary?"

"Yes, I do."

"So, anyone viewing this who agrees with me is also a traitor?"

"Yes."

"Do you think that coming on this programme today and vigorously defending the brutality of your regime is going to endear you to a worried nation?"

"The nation is not worried; only a few liberals with weak stomachs are. It is really so simple, Sara, that even you should understand. I was voted in to cut crime, and I have done so."

"Let me just ensure I understand this. Anyone like me who feels Aaron Davis' execution is wrong is a traitor and a liberal with a weak stomach. Yes or no?"

"Yes."

"On that note, we have run out of time. Certainly, Prime Minister, you have defended your position extremely strongly today. We shall find out in the coming days, through opinion polls, how your tough message has gone down with the electorate. Thank you for coming in and talking to us so frankly."

"Thank you for inviting me."

"I will be back at the same time tomorrow. If you would like to comment on anything said in today's show, the contact details will be on screen after the credits. Thank you for watching and goodbye."

For a few seconds, there is silence then the crew and executives watching in the studio burst into spontaneous applause.

William Marshall descends on the prime minister and shakes his hand warmly. "Brilliant. Great TV. Well done, both of you. Just like two prize fighters slugging it out to the final bell. Sir, you are welcome back at any time. Perhaps you could give us an exclusive interview in the run up to the next general election?"

Bob ignores the question and turns to Sara. "I thought you were going to be gentle."

It is William Marshall who answers: "That was gentle."

Sara intervenes, explaining, "The country saw the true Bob Godwin today: passionate, hard-working and doing what he thinks is best for the country. That would never have happened if I had been gentle."

The prime minister doesn't seem convinced, but he joins in the small talk for a few minutes before departing.

Sara asks, "What does social media think?"

Mr Marshall replies, "That he is a ruthless, heartless dictator who blames everybody but himself. You were brilliant. He didn't even feel the sting. We are going to devote tomorrow's programme to the viewer's reactions. Join us all later for a celebration drink. You are simply a star."

"I will see how I feel later. I will need to do some research before tomorrow, but we'll see."

*

A few minutes later, Sara is in her dressing room. Her mobile shows three missed calls and a message, all from Bob. She listens to the message: "Sara, hi. I think that went really well. Please come over tonight, and we will celebrate. Bring a bag and stay overnight."

Sara deletes the message and switches the phone off.

*

The next day, the interview is front-page headline news. None of the major daily papers have a good word to say about the prime minister. "Child beater", "Scum" and "You were better when you were a recluse, Mr Godwin" are just three of the headlines. Sara comes out unscathed from the various press critiques.

"Sara Molan, fifteen; Sue Horton, fifteen. Molan to serve," she says out loud.

A quick check of her phone shows five missed calls and another message, which she deletes without hearing what Bob has to say.

Sara's show that day simply rubs salt in the wounds. It includes many phone calls, half a dozen emails and some social media comments; every single one of them criticising the prime minister for his intransigence, his bloodthirstiness and his total lack of sympathy for those worse off than him, along with many other perceived faults in his character or behaviour.

William Marshall arrives as the programme ends and approaches Sara the second she comes off air. "Will you spare me a few minutes in the next week or so? I think we need to discuss a new contract for you and extending the show by, say, fifteen minutes a day."

"Um, yes… yes, of course. Ask your secretary to send me a few possible dates and times, and I'll pick one that suits me too. Um, thank you."

She waits for the executive to disappear from sight before allowing a broad smile to cross her face, and she thinks to herself, *I love it when a plan comes together.*

CHAPTER 10

PRECIOUS

NOVEMBER 2032 – MAY 2033

Precious Matale is twenty-five years old and works as a healthcare assistant at Belford Hospital in Fort William, Scotland. She is single, deeply religious and strongly disapproves of sex outside marriage.

Like all unmarried women, she is forced to undergo an annual virginity test, something she finds painful, intrusive and embarrassing. Despite these misgivings, Precious visits a nurse at her GP's surgery for the examination. She is totally shocked to be told that she has failed the test. The nurse is sympathetic, but she tells the weeping patient that, by law, she must inform the police. Whilst they are waiting for the officers, another nurse carries out the test and confirms that medically speaking, she is no longer a virgin.

The police arrive and take her to the police station, where she is examined and tested yet again by a police doctor. Precious is charged with failing a virginity test and having sex whilst unmarried.

She appears briefly in court the next day and pleads not guilty. Precious is remanded on unconditional bail to appear in court at Fort William in four weeks' time. She also decides to employ a solicitor to fight her case. As soon as the details of the case appear in the *Fort William Herald*, she is suspended from work – fortunately, on full pay. At her solicitor's request, Precious gets statements from her friends and colleagues confirming that they have never seen Precious with a boyfriend and that she has never mentioned sexual activity to them.

*

In early January 2033, she appears in court for the actual trial. The prosecution calls the police doctor to confirm he carried out a virginity test on Ms Matale and that she failed the test. The prosecutor also reads out statements from the two nurses at the defendant's surgery confirming that they, too, carried out tests that show Precious is no longer a virgin in medical terms. The prosecution then rests their case.

The defence case opens with the defence solicitor, Hugh McGarvey, calling Precious to the stand to give evidence in her defence.

"Ms Matale, let us get straight to the point here. Have you ever had sexual relations with another person?" he enquires.

"No, I have not," Precious confirms.

"Have you ever given yourself sexual pleasure?"

"No."

"Do you agree with sex before marriage?"

"No, I do not. I am a God-fearing, devout Christian. The Bible says that sex should only take place between man and wife. I would never go against the teachings of the Bible."

"Do you have any idea how you have failed three virginity tests?"

"None at all."

"Do you keep fit or take regular exercise?"

"I cycle everywhere, and I play netball twice a week."

"Thank you. No more questions."

The sheriff asks the prosecution if they have any questions.

"No, Your Honour," the prosecution responds.

The sheriff tells Precious she can stand down.

"The defence rests," concludes Mr McGarvey.

"In that case," says the sheriff. "The prosecution can present its summing up."

The prosecution duly obliges: "Your Honour, this is not a complex case. We have heard evidence from three medical professionals that Ms Matale is not a virgin. The law states that all unmarried women must pass a virginity test annually. If they do not take or fail the test, then they are automatically considered by the law to be engaging in sexual relations outside the sanctity of marriage. This is a criminal offence under the law, and the penalty for this offence is a mandatory sentence of at least 1,000 strokes of the nine-tailed whip, plus if the court so wishes, a jail term or a fine or both."

Precious looks shaken in the dock and starts to weep quietly.

"Mr McGarvey, I imagine you wish to say something at this point," offers the sheriff.

"Yes, Your Honour. The prosecution has offered evidence about the failed tests but not a single shred of proof that these results were due to sexual activity. Ms Matale is deeply religious, and for her to lie – having sworn an oath on the Bible – is just implausible. I have presented to the court in advance of this hearing a number of testimonies affirming the defendant's lack of boyfriends, and that she has frequently told her friends and colleagues that she is strongly against premarital sexual activity. My client cycles on a daily basis and also partakes in sport. These activities can damage the hymen and produce exactly the same internal appearance as a female who has partaken in sexual relations. There are many reports from reputable organisations over the last few decades stating how unreliable these tests are. Until a change of government in London in 2029, the UK was a leading critic of other countries still using virginity testing. The Justice Act 2029, which does cover Scottish cases in this matter, introduced these unreliable, hated tests into this country under the guise of law and order. This country now finds itself on the other side of the argument, with many countries urging us to ban this discredited, humiliating process immediately. Your Honour, these tests can and do lie. Deeply religious women like Ms Matale do not lie when they have taken an oath on the Holy Bible to tell the truth, the whole truth and nothing but the truth. I urge the court to throw out these ridiculous charges."

"Thank you, Mr McGarvey," responds the sheriff. "I wish to retire to consult the actual wording of the relevant act and also to look at any case law on this subject. Court is adjourned."

Precious and her solicitor leave the courtroom and go outside, where they linger in the cold winter air, awaiting developments. After about ten minutes, they are called back into court to hear the sheriff's verdict.

"Ms Matale, I believe that you are telling the truth," the sheriff declares once they are all settled back in the courtroom. "I also accept that these tests have a very chequered record of accuracy and that other factors such as sport, cycling and strenuous exercise can also produce an incorrect result where no sexual activity has taken place. However, this is a court of law. The relevant law here is the Justice Act 2029. This act states, as the prosecutor mentioned earlier, that a failed virginity test alone is sufficient for a defendant to be found guilty, not only of not passing the test but also of unlawful sexual activity. I have, on previous occasions, expressed my deep opposition to clauses contained within this act, but there seems no government willingness to redraft it or repeal it altogether. I reluctantly, and in no way whatsoever as a reflection of the defendant's honesty or reputation, find Ms Matale guilty of both charges. Mr McGarvey, before I pass sentence may I ask you, please, for information about the security of your client's employment?"

"Yes, Your Honour. Ms Matale is presently suspended from work. She will automatically lose her job if she is given an immediate term of imprisonment or is sentenced to more than 1,000 strokes of the nine-tailed whip," Mr Garvey confirms.

"Thank you, Mr McGarvey. Ms Matale, I believe your testimony, but my hands are tied by the law – however unfair, brutal and ridiculous it may be. I can offer little comfort to you as I have no option but to sentence you to 1,000 strokes of the nine-tailed whip. This punishment is mandatory, and I have no discretion over it. I also sentence you to six months' imprisonment, suspended for one year. You cannot be prosecuted again for these offences, so if you do not get into any other trouble in the next twelve months, the prison term will be cancelled automatically. This sentence, whilst painful and difficult for you to accept, will enable you to continue in your job without further sanctions against you."

Mr McGarvey rises. "Your Honour, I would like permission to appeal."

"Permission refused. Do you think I would inflict any of this on your client if there were any alternative? The law is the law. The Justice Act is actually written in clear language. There is no hope of misinterpreting it. If a single female fails the annual virginity test, she is automatically guilty of the offence of having sex whilst unmarried. This whole Act is a disaster and criminalises totally innocent people, but as I just said, the law is the law, unfortunately. I have been as lenient as I possibly can be. If you appeal, you will lose. The Appeal Court may not look as kindly upon your client as I do. Case closed."

*

After discussions with her employers and solicitors, Precious decides reluctantly to accept the sentence of the court and keep her job, despite still maintaining her innocence. Before any punishment can be administered, she must attend Inverness Punishment Centre for a medical examination. The doctor there considers that Precious is at risk if she receives her full punishment in one session and so decides that she should receive 250 strokes at each of four sessions, which are to be at least four weeks apart.

This proves to be to her advantage, as in fact, she does not suffer too badly at each session and is able to work some shifts between the punishments, which Belford Hospital are happy to agree to due to staff shortages and severe winter pressures.

In May, she finally completes her punishment, and she tells the *Fort William Herald* that she wishes to put the whole thing behind her and, as a practising Christian, she bears no grudges against anyone for her ordeal.

*

Sara Molan manages to avoid Bob Godwin's calls and messages for several months after their fateful interview. Finally, he tricks her by using a different phone.

"What the hell were you playing at, making me look like a bloodthirsty tyrant?" he demands.

"I thought you did that perfectly well without any help from me," Sara retorts.

"Don't you talk to me like that. What do you think all the flowers and chocolates were for?"

"To get me into bed with you."

"Well, that too. You were supposed to be on my side, and you let me down. You owe me and you will repay me."

"What does that mean?"

"I want to do one more interview, next April when Parliament dissolves before the general election. You will do that interview on my terms. I will write the questions beforehand, and you will say nothing during the interview except reading your script. No snide remarks, no disputing my answers, no sarcastic comments – nothing. Do you understand?"

"I understand, but even if I were prepared to work that way, my boss won't be. If you want a lap dog to interview you, I'll get you Sue Horton's number. She'll probably make you a lovely hand-knitted pullover to wear during the interview as a bonus."

"You know I only want you. And you can tell Marshall that I want a written agreement from him in the next month. If not, I will tell the Metropolitan Police commissioner about a little redhead called Suzi. I am sure he will understand. And by the way, do not think for a minute that I don't have all the dirt on you, young lady. I know why you left India, I know all about your sordid little affair with Nic, and I am quite happy to have you called in for a nice little virginity test."

"So, the great Bob Godwin is nothing but a blackmailing loser."

"Oh no, darling, you are the loser. I am the winner. I am calling the shots now."

"But this is ridiculous. There's well over a year to the next general election. I could be working in a different country by then."

"Not with that brand new, fat contract in your back pocket, you won't be. Of course, you might be dead."

"Are you threatening me?"

"Not at all. I'm just reminding you that you need to be careful not to upset anyone important in the next twelve months or so. Politics can be so dangerous, I always feel. Oh, and there are a few other conditions to next year's interview: it will take place in Downing Street, you will come alone and you will not be leaving until the next day. Bring some sexy underwear."

"You're mad. William Marshall will never agree to any of this."

"Do not forget to tell him he has a month to put this in writing. Otherwise, the pair of you will find out just how nasty I can be. Bye, darling. See you next year. Have a safe life."

*

"No! Over my dead body." William Marshall smashes his fist into his desk. "You are not doing an interview in Downing Street alone with that maniac."

"I don't think we've got much choice, have we? I can look after myself, and there are bound to be people in Downing Street, even in the run up to a general election. I can scream very loudly when I have to. He said that if you were reluctant, I should mention a little redhead called Suzi," Sara says cautiously, unsure of her boss's reaction.

"Shit. How the hell does he know about that?"

"Don't ask me. I don't know anything about any Suzi, so there is no way I could have told him. He knows everything. He knows about my past in India, which I am not ashamed of, but I have never mentioned it to anyone in this country. He even knows about my new contract. I think that, at the moment, we need to agree to what he says and hope that events in the next twelve months will help us avoid having to go through with it."

"And if we don't agree?"

"I think we could both have very sore bottoms before we are much older. Not to mention the beautiful brandings on our foreheads."

"Sara, it's you who will be at the mercy of this lunatic. Are you sure you want to agree to this?"

"Just send him the confirmation he wants and pray to your God for a miracle. A plague of locusts next March or April would be brilliant. It will all be fine," Sara declares, trying to sound more confident than she feels.

*

A brief text arrives on her phone a few days later: "That's a date then. Don't forget the underwear. Of course, if you can't wait until 2034, just give me a ring."

Sara immediately dials a number, but only gets through to an answering machine. "Nic, we might be about to be exposed. I hope you haven't been opening your mouth to the wrong people. Please ring me. I miss you and I need to talk to you."

An hour later, her phone rings and Sara answers the call joyfully. "Nic, how are you?"

"I'm fine. You didn't sound on the message as if you are," replies a familiar voice.

"Oh, it's just politics. Someone claims to know about us. I just wanted to warn you really."

"And to make sure I haven't been opening my mouth."

"Please, Nic, let's not fall out."

"I thought we did that four years ago. For the record, I have not spoken to anyone about you. Here, nobody knows who you are, anyway."

"Where's here?"

"Marseilles."

"Sounds great."

"It is. You are welcome to join me if you are in any trouble."

"No, no; honestly, I'm fine. I don't think any secrets are going to come out now anyway. I felt I should tell you, just in case. Nic, I still love you. Do you think we could try again sometime?"

"I honestly don't know, Sara. I'd like to think we could. Let's keep in touch and let's be friends. I can't promise more than that."

"That's more than fair. I'll ring you. Bye."

GOVERNMENT PRONOUNCEMENTS

November 2032: All private ownership of guns is prohibited immediately.

December 2032: All supermarkets and shops are forbidden to sell more than one item of confectionery per customer, to assist with government plans to encourage citizens to eat more healthily.

January 2033: A new national register of all knife sales is to be set up as a matter of urgency.

February 2033: There is to be no new immigration, apart from those immigrants who have needed skills and a guaranteed job to go to in this country.

May 2033: Any foreign nationals convicted in court of criminal offences are to be sentenced to imprisonment and deported at the end of their sentence. There are to be immediate tax rises of 5%.

CHAPTER 11

JERRY

MAY 2033 – NOVEMBER 2033

Jerry O'Brien is fifty-one years old and lives a peaceful life in rural Yorkshire with his wife of thirty years (Arlene) and two dogs. His two children have moved out of the family home but are still in regular contact. Their eight-year-old grandson is currently living with them. Everybody loves Jerry. As well as holding down a full-time job as a postman, he is a pillar of the community, serving on the local council and volunteering with various local projects that help underprivileged children. He is used to the local community police officer calling on him to discuss problems with specific youngsters, so he is totally unconcerned when two detectives visit in early May.

"Are you Jerry O'Brien?" asks the older of the policemen.

"Oh, come on, Doug. You know I am," replies Jerry.

"I would like you to come with us to the police station, please."

"Are you arresting me?" Jerry asks, shocked by the way this conversation is going. "Whatever for? I've done nothing."

"You're not under arrest. We would just like you to come with us so we can ask you a few questions."

"Do I need a solicitor?"

"Well, that's up to you, but I think you should seriously consider it."

"Arlene, I've got to go to the police station. Ring Paul Flaherty and get him to meet me there."

*

At the police station, Jerry is treated well, and about two hours later, he is seated in an interview room with his solicitor, Detective Sergeant [DS] Ed Jenkins and Detective Constable [DC] Jamie Harrison."

"Interview with Jerry O'Brien, commencing at 3.05pm on 10th May 2033," DS Jenkins says formally.

"What on earth is all this about?" queries Jerry.

"We are investigating allegations of the sexual abuse of children at community camps in this area about thirty years ago," DS Jenkins explains. "Did you act as a helper at such camps?"

Paul Flaherty turns to his client and says, "Jerry, you do not have to answer any questions if you do not want to."

"No, I want to cooperate. I have nothing at all to hide. Anyway, they can ask anyone about this. It is common knowledge that I and many others used to help at these camps, if you can call them that. A group of volunteers used to take some of the local youngsters out into the woods to stay over for a few days and nights. It was like Scout camp without the uniforms. There have been some rumours in the past about so-called 'incidents', but nothing has ever come of it, because nothing ever happened."

"Can you confirm that, in August 2001, you took part in a community camp over four days in Metlock Woods?"

"I have no idea about the date, but we used to stay in those woods sometimes, and if there was a camp at that time, then I would have been there. I went to all of them between 1999 and 2003, when the camps came to an end."

"Why did they stop?"

"I had met my future wife. Most of the other volunteers were around my age. We were all settling down with partners and starting families. We had too much else to do. There was nothing suspicious about the camps ending."

"Yet you said earlier there were rumours flying around."

"That came later. Look, some of the boys had their fathers with them."

"So, this was an all-male affair?"

"It was an all-male get-together to teach basic survival methods and do various activities in the countryside."

"Including abusing small boys?"

Peter Flaherty intervenes, "Don't answer that."

DS Jenkins tries another approach: "What exactly was your role at these camps?"

"I just helped out. I did whatever needed to be done," Jerry answers.

"Where did you sleep?"

"In my own tent."

"And the boys?"

"We used to take twelve boys at a time, and we provided six tents. So, two boys shared each tent."

"Did you ever enter any of the boys' tents?"

"Sometimes, I suppose. If they were late for an activity or there was some kind of emergency."

"Do you remember going into one of the tents at Metlock Woods in August 2001?"

"Of course I don't. It was over thirty years ago." Jerry stops and confers with his solicitor at this point.

Peter Flaherty then addresses DS Jenkins: "My client categorically denies any abuse of children at the community camps he attended. He is unable to account for his precise actions due to the decades that have passed since the camps took place. I have advised my client not to answer any further questions. You know Mr O'Brien's position on this matter, and it is effectively his word against whatever evidence you feel you have. So, it is up to you. Arrest him or release him."

"In that case, Jerry O'Brien, I am charging you with two counts of indecent assault on boys aged under ten years of age," concludes DS Jenkins.

With that, Jerry is handed over to the custody sergeant and appears in court the next morning, where he is given unconditional bail until the trial six weeks hence.

*

At the trial, Jerry enters formal pleas of not guilty to both charges.

The prosecutor, Mr Quinton, then proceeds to outline the case against Mr O'Brien: "These charges arise from incidents at a community camp in August 2001. The defendant was a volunteer helper at the camp, which was attended by twelve local boys aged between eight and ten years old. There were twelve boys and six tents, so two boys were assigned to each tent. The two complainants in this case were both aged eight years old at the time of the alleged offences and were sharing a tent that was adjacent to a single tent occupied by the defendant. The prosecution's case is that, at about 6.30am on the final day of the camp, the defendant entered the tent nearest to his own and woke up both occupants. One of the boys was ordered by the defendant to go to the showers. The defendant then told the remaining boy to take off his pyjama trousers, and it is alleged he indecently assaulted the boy. When the first boy returned he, too, was assaulted in front of the first victim. In view of the nature of this case, it has been agreed that the complainants will give evidence behind screens in order to conceal their identity. I call my first witness, who is to be known as Witness A."

When the witness has got into place behind the screens and been sworn in, Mr Quinton asks him what happened on the 2001 camp.

"It was the last morning, and I was asleep when I felt someone shaking me," explains Witness A. "It was Jerry. He had already woken up my tent mate. He told the other boy to go and have a shower and come straight back to the tent. He then told me to get out of bed. I was feeling quite worried, and I was afraid to get out. Jerry grabbed me and hauled me out of bed. He seemed quite angry. He told me to take off my pyjama trousers. I was terrified not to, as he seemed so mad. He then touched me on my penis and kissed me on the mouth. He then knelt down and sucked my penis several times. He then told me to get dressed and not to tell anyone or I would get in serious trouble. At that point, the other boy came in, and Jerry did exactly the same to him. Then he told us to go back to bed, and he left the tent."

"You are unable to see the defendant, but you have been shown recent photographs of him. Are you sure this is the same person who was in the tent that morning?" queries Mr Quinton.

"Yes, I am."

"Even though the incident was over thirty years ago?"

"I will never forget his face."

"Thank you. No further questions."

The judge speaks next: "Mr Flaherty. Do you have any questions for this witness?"

"Yes, I do." Mr Flaherty turns to where the witness is behind the screen. "This is all nonsense, isn't it? A pack of lies from start to finish."

"No. I am telling the truth."

"That you can identify now someone you saw in half-light, at best, some thirty years ago?"

"I could see his face, but I also knew his voice. He'd been talking to us and living next to us for three days and nights. It was Jerry."

"But is it the same Jerry in the recent photographs of the defendant?"

"Yes."

"How can you possibly be sure after so much time has passed?"

"I have never forgotten that face. He has aged and changed, but that is the same person who attacked me that morning."

"What educational qualifications do you have?"

"None. I was never the same after that camp. I couldn't concentrate on anything."

"Do you work?"

"Not at the moment."

"Have you ever worked?"

"Occasionally, but I lose confidence and concentration."

"So, you live on benefits and cannot hold down a job, and it is all because of something you claim happened over three decades ago."

"Yes."

"Unbelievable."

"It's the truth."

"Your version of it, perhaps."

"Objection," says Mr Quinton, rising from his chair.

"Sustained," confirms the judge.

"No more questions, Your Honour," responds Mr Flaherty.

"The witness may stand down. Do you wish to call another witness, Mr Quinton?"

"Yes, Your Honour. I wish to call Witness B."

After the usual preliminaries, the prosecutor starts questioning the new witness: "Please tell the court your recollections of the events in the early morning of your last day at camp in August 2001."

Witness B begins, "I was asleep and felt someone shaking me. At first, I couldn't see who it was. Then he spoke to me, and I recognised the voice as that of Jerry, one of the helpers at the camp. He told me to get up, and he went over to the other boy in the tent and started shaking him. He told me to go and have a shower and come straight back to the tent. I did as he said. When I came back, the other boy looked shaken and was pulling up his pyjamas. I was very frightened. Jerry told me to take off my pyjama trousers and stand in front of him. He held my penis and sort of squeezed it and at the same time he kissed me on the lips. I tried to back away, but he grabbed me, bent over and put my penis in his mouth. I started to cry, and he let me go. He told me not to tell anyone or I would be in trouble and nobody would believe me."

"What contact have you had with the other witness since 2001?"

"Very little. We went to different schools and had different friends. We lived in a small town, so we saw each other occasionally in the street or at a café. I saw in the paper that the police were investigating abuse at the community camps and decided I should tell them what happened to me."

"How has the attack affected you?"

"Very little. It crosses my mind once in a while, but that's all."

"Are you 100% sure that the defendant is the person who assaulted you?"

"Yes."

"Thank you. No more questions."

Mr Flaherty rises and speaks to the witness. "You say that you came forward after seeing that the police were investigating incidents at the camps."

"Yes," Witness B confirms.

"Were you aware that there had been two previous investigations into these matters?"

"Yes, I was."

"So why did you not come forward, then?"

"I don't know really. I didn't want to get involved, I guess."

"What is different now?"

"It just seemed the right thing to do."

"The fact that you have a newspaper interview lined up if my client is convicted, with a fee of £1,000, has nothing to do with you being here today peddling lies?"

"Nothing at all."

"No more questions, Your Honour." With that, Mr Flaherty sits back down.

"I have another question," says Mr Quinton, rising from his seat once more.

"When you first contacted the police with your evidence, had you been contacted by the newspaper my learned colleague mentioned?"

"No. The interview offer came later."

"Thank you. No more questions. The case for the prosecution is closed."

Mr Flaherty gets back to his feet. "The defence wishes to call only one witness: the defendant, Jerry O'Brien."

After the witness preliminaries are complete, the solicitor asks his first question. "Did you attend a community camp in August 2001 in Metlock Woods?"

"Yes, I did," states Jerry.

"In what capacity?"

"As a voluntary helper. I just did whatever needed to be done and generally made sure everything went smoothly."

"Did you ever need to go into the tents as part of your duties?"

"Sometimes, if someone was late or if there was a problem."

"Do you remember going into a tent very early in the morning on the last day of that camp?"

"I have no recollection of that specifically, but I definitely did not enter any tents early in the morning. I might have done so if someone was not up and about at, say, 8am."

"Did you ever tell one boy in a tent to go and have a shower, leaving you alone with the other boy?"

"No."

"Did you ever ask or tell a boy to take off his pyjama trousers?"

"Definitely not."

"Did you ever touch or indecently assault any boy?"

"Categorically not."

"Have you ever been in trouble with the law?"

"Never. I've not even had a parking ticket."

"Until this case, have you ever been asked any questions by the police about these camps?"

"There have been some rumours going around for years about problems at the camps, but to the best of my knowledge, this is the first time anything official has happened. It has got nothing at all to do with me."

"Are you married, Mr O'Brien?"

"Yes, for thirty years."

"Any children?"

"Two."

"Any grandchildren?"

"One."

"So, you have a happy family life, no criminal record and like to help out by volunteering locally in your spare time, assisting at community events such as the camps. Hardly the normal profile of a paedophile."

"Objection," Mr Quinton calls out.

"Sustained. Ask a question, Mr Flaherty," commands the judge.

"Did you commit the offences you are charged with?" Mr Flaherty asks.

"No, I did not. I would never do anything like that. I find the whole idea totally disgusting."

"Thank you, Mr O'Brien."

The judge asks Mr Quinton, "Any questions for the defendant?"

"No, Your Honour," he confirms.

"You may stand down, Mr O'Brien. Mr Quinton, do you want to make the closing statement for the prosecution?"

"Certainly, Your Honour. There is a misconception concerning historic sex abuse cases. It is taken for granted that memories will fade and distort what actually occurred. It is clear from the evidence of the two alleged victims that the events of that early morning visit are as vivid in their memories as on the day it took place. There are two witnesses and two consistent stories against one defendant, who cannot or will not offer any information about the events on that day. Two eight-year-old boys were abused that day by a man they knew as Jerry. It is correct to say that one of those boys has been traumatised for life by the events that took place in a tent at the community camp. They have identified recent photographs of the defendant as their attacker that day. Your Honour, there are no other witnesses and no forensic evidence, but we have consistent stories, ongoing after-effects and the positive identification of the attacker. I ask you to return a verdict of guilty, so the offender can be punished, the victims can have closure, and two wrongs can be put right."

"Mr Flaherty," prompts the judge.

"There is a difference between remembering events from long ago and making up a false memory. These are two witnesses with identical stories that are backed up by absolutely nothing. One witness – who has achieved little, if anything, in his life – is blaming anyone but himself for his problems. The second witness chose to say nothing for over thirty years, but now has a nice little contract with a newspaper for his story – though, of course, he needs someone to be convicted first. The defendant, on the other hand, is a man of unblemished character, a pillar of his community, a loving member of a long-established marriage and a family man. Mr O'Brien also strongly denies the allegations and, indeed, says he is disgusted by them. It does not matter that he cannot recall every move he made on a day over thirty years ago. He remembers that he did not assault two young boys and has said so under oath. Your Honour, I ask you to ensure justice is done here by acquitting my client of all charges against him."

The judge addresses the two counsels: "I feel I need some time in my chambers to go over this case. The court is adjourned until I arrive at a verdict."

*

It is over an hour before the court reconvenes.

The judge begins to deliver the verdict immediately: "Cases involving incidents from decades ago always cause difficulties for judges. Time does affect memories, take away witnesses and make the truth hard to arrive at. In the end, I can only reach a decision on whom I believe is telling the truth and whom has reason to lie. I am concerned, like Mr Flaherty, at the virtually identical accounts of the incident by the two witnesses. Of course, they may have superb memories, but there may be suggestions of collusion here. I also feel concern whenever it is revealed that a witness is planning to make money by selling their story once a guilty verdict has occurred. The defendant has no previous convictions and appears to live a settled, blameless life, both inside and outside of his own family unit. Cases like this are never black and white. On the basis of what has been said in this courtroom during Mr O'Brien's trial, I consider the only just verdict is to find the defendant not guilty on all charges against him. Mr O'Brien, you are free to leave this court without a stain on your reputation."

Jerry shakes Mr Flaherty's hand robustly and smiles broadly.

*

That evening. Jerry goes into his grandson's room to say goodnight. "Hi Jamie, did you remember what I said to you this morning?"

"Yes, Grandad. I didn't put my pyjama trousers on."

*

The two complainants face charges of falsely making claims of sexual abuse and are convicted of that offence at a later trial. They are each sentenced to the minimum punishment of 500 strokes of the nine-tailed whip.

*

Sara has become used to receiving regular texts from Bob stating how many days are left before the interview. She deletes the latest with a sigh and tries to concentrate on something – anything – else.

GOVERNMENT PRONOUNCEMENTS

November 2033: The general election date is confirmed for the first Thursday in May 2034. Crime is down 68%

since the last general election. The age of consent and the age at which citizens may marry, with or without their parents' consent, is to increase immediately to twenty years of age. The age at which citizens are eligible to apply for a driving license is to increase to nineteen years of age.

CHAPTER 12

KATRINA

NOVEMBER 2033 – FEBRUARY 2034

In November 2033, Katrina Miller is forty-two years old and celebrating twenty years of marriage to her husband, James.

Unfortunately, the marriage has been going through a rough patch. So rough, in fact, that Mr Miller has hired a private investigator to find out why his wife is spending so much of her time away from home. The investigator follows Katrina to a hotel, where she has lunch with a man. After finishing eating, they retire to a room at the hotel, emerging separately about three hours later.

*

The following week, the same happens, but this time the private detective is not alone. James Miller has contacted the police, and about fifteen minutes after Mrs Miller and her companion enter room twenty-two, three officers break into the room and catch the couple having sex.

At the police station, the truth emerges. Katrina has been having an affair for over two years with her unmarried boss, Richard Addison. Katrina is charged with adultery and her lover is charged with having sex whilst unmarried.

*

In early December, Katrina and Richard appear together in court. Both admit the charges facing them. Richard is sentenced to four years imprisonment and 1,000 strokes of the nine-tailed whip. Judge Robertson decides he wants to hold a sentencing hearing for Mrs Miller on Christmas Eve. She is remanded to prison, as the judge tells her that a lengthy term of imprisonment is inevitable. He also requests physical and mental reports before deciding on Katrina's punishment.

*

As previously arranged, Katrina appears in court again for sentencing on 24th December. Her husband, James, is seated prominently in the public gallery, along with their teenage daughter, Madeleine.

The prosecutor, Mr Philip Forrest KC, addresses Judge Robertson first: "This is an extremely serious case involving, as the defendant, a married woman who was conducting a lengthy affair with her unmarried boss. Mrs Miller was caught in bed having sexual intercourse with Mr Richard Addison. At the time, she was – and still is – legally married to James Miller and was living with her husband. Whilst, historically, adultery has mainly been considered to be against moral and religious teachings in this country, the law has changed under our present government. Adultery is now a criminal offence, punishable by severe penalties. In order to commit this offence, the defendant has lied to her husband and daughter over a lengthy period, apparently without a care for anyone but herself. I ask the court to consider a sentence significantly above the starting level here of twelve years' imprisonment, branding and 1,000 strokes of the nine-tailed whip."

A loud gasp is heard from Madeleine in the gallery, and Katrina slumps in her chair.

The defence barrister, Mrs Eileen Jarvis KC, stands and speaks directly to the judge: "Your Honour, my client freely admits her guilt, and she did so at the earliest possible opportunity. Her worst punishment is the distress she has caused to her daughter and husband, for whom she still has feelings. Her daughter is eighteen years old and entering a period of her life where she will doubtless miss her mother's presence and advice. Mrs Miller got caught in a situation she desperately wanted to escape from, but could never manage to do so. She has asked me specifically to apologise to the court for her actions and to her family for the worry she has put them through. The defendant is not the cold-hearted human being suggested by my learned counsel, the prosecutor. She is a deeply embarrassed and ashamed woman who wishes she could turn back the clock. I appreciate that there are mandatory minimum sentences pertaining to the offence of adultery. Even so, I ask on behalf of my client that you are as lenient as possible. No punishment can make her feel any worse than she does at this time. Thank you, Your Honour."

"I am going to adjourn this court and consider the best way forward here. Please take the prisoner to the cells," declares the judge.

*

About thirty minutes later, two female court officers enter Katrina's cell.

One says, "Miller, get all your clothes off. By order of the judge."

"What? Why on earth do I have to strip? Am I expected to appear in court naked in front of my daughter and everyone else in there? No way. I want my solicitor," Katrina responds.

The officers withdraw and return a few minutes later with Mrs Jarvis. They all enter the cell.

"What on earth is happening, Eileen?" asks Katrina, upset and close to tears.

"I've spoken to the judge," confirms Eileen. "He says he has the right to publicly humiliate prisoners whom he intends to pass heavy sentences on. He is adamant that you either appear naked for sentencing or he will double all parts of the sentence he intends to give you. I suspect he is thinking way above the minimum. Even if he is planning on passing the lowest sentence, it will be twelve years and 1,000 strokes of the nine-tailed whip. Do I need to spell out to you what double that amounts to?"

"He can't do this to me. He just can't. Surely we can appeal?" wails Katrina.

"We can't appeal now to stop him having you naked. His court, his rules. You can stay here and have your sentence doubled. We can appeal that, but in the present judicial climate, I am not prepared to give you any realistic hope of success. You could end up spending the next thirty or forty years behind bars and with so much flogging that you will undoubtedly suffer permanent injury. I have never come across anything else like this. Welcome to Common Sense justice."

"Come on, Miller, decide what to do. We haven't got all day," demands one of the officers.

Katrina is crying uncontrollably by now and does not reply, but she starts unbuttoning her prison-uniform blouse.

*

Her entrance into the dock causes shock amongst the people watching the sentencing. Madeleine bursts into tears and buries her head in her father's lap.

When the judge enters the court, he orders Katrina to stand, exposing her fully to the people present. Tears are pouring down her face, and one of the officers guarding her has to give her a tissue.

Judge Robertson begins, "I have given instructions that the defendant should appear naked for sentencing. There are two reasons for this. One is humiliation. Nobody wants to be shamed like this. I want the prisoner to remember this throughout the serving of her sentence. The second reason is that I have decided that Mrs Miller's crime deserves severe retribution with regular corporal punishment. She may as well get used to being without clothes, as her beatings will no doubt limit her ability to get dressed for long periods whilst in prison. The reports I ordered show no physical impediments to corporal punishment. There is some concern about the defendant's mental state, which is probably driven by guilt. She will have plenty of time to think about her crime and the tsunami of misery she has unleashed through her actions. With regard to sentencing, I am far more inclined to agree with Mr Forrest, and his request for a higher penalty than the mandatory minimum sentence, than I am to acquiesce to Mrs Jarvis' pleas for clemency. I sentence Mrs Katrina Miller to the following punishment: fifteen years' imprisonment, a total of 750 cane strokes on her bare buttocks, 750 cane strokes on her bare breasts, 2,000 strokes of the nine-tailed whip on her bare back and branding on the forehead as an adulteress."

There is an immediate uproar in the court as Madeleine bursts into tears and shouts, "*No. No. That's my mother.*"

Katrina crumples in the dock, struggling for breath. The officers grab her and stop her hitting the floor.

"*Silence!*" shouts the judge, banging his gavel. "Usher, clear the court. Take the prisoner to the cells."

Mrs Jarvis rises. "Your Honour, with your permission, I would like to visit my client in the cells. I am worried about her collapse in the dock and would like to make sure she is receiving appropriate treatment."

"Yes, of course you have my permission. I am not hard-hearted, you know."

*

It is about thirty minutes before the barrister enters Katrina's cell. Her client is still naked, although she is now covered by a blanket. She is now breathing more easily, but still crying.

"How are you?" Eileen enquires.

"Bloody awful. How do you think I am? Fifteen years, 2,000 lashes and, as if that weren't enough for the bastard, 1,500 strokes with the cane. He isn't even satisfied with seeing my tits; he wants to tear them apart as well," Katrina says.

"It is a dreadfully severe sentence. We can appeal. At the moment, though, I'm more worried about your health. Have you had any treatment?"

"No, but there is supposed to be a doctor coming to look at me. I'm breathing better now. I think it was just a shock. I knew I would be jailed and beaten, but I never expected that much severity."

"Do you think you should go to hospital?"

"I don't know; I don't feel too good."

Mrs Jarvis calls for assistance and discusses the situation with the court officer who responds to her request for help. It is decided that the safest thing is to take Katrina to hospital under guard for assessment. Fortunately, or perhaps unfortunately for Katrina, the doctors in the hospital could not find anything seriously wrong, and later that day, she is transferred to prison.

*

For the first two weeks, Mrs Miller is just allowed to settle into prison routine. On the fifteenth day of her sentence, things change markedly. Before breakfast, a warder enters Katrina's cell and tells her not to eat or drink anything as she is going to be punished today. At about 9am, two female guards enter and handcuff her to the wrist of one of the guards. They take her out of the cell, and then – with much locking and unlocking of doors – march her out of the main entrance of the prison and into a van.

"Where are we going?" asks Katrina as the guards handcuff her to a post in the back of the van.

"Punishment centre," one of them replies flatly.

"What am I getting?" There is a distinct nervousness in the prisoner's voice now.

"No idea. We take you there, we watch you getting beaten and then we bring you back."

*

About twenty minutes pass before the van stops, and soon the guards open up the back of the van and release Katrina briefly before handcuffing her to one of the guards, as previously. When they step out of the van, Mrs Miller finds herself in an underground car park. She has no choice but to walk the same way as the woman she is shackled to.

At the end of the car park, there is a door with a buzzer, which the guard with two free hands presses.

An unseen voice responds, "Who's there?"

"Prison detail with Katrina Miller," announces the same guard.

The door buzzes, the guard opens it, and the three women go through into a brightly lit corridor. An arrow on the wall points to reception, and that is the way they go.

Another door and buzzer await the trio. Having successfully passed through this obstacle, they are now in a wider corridor with a desk at the far end. There is no one their side of the desk, but a young woman sits behind it, staring down at a piece of paper.

In a few seconds, they are facing the receptionist,

who wears a badge bearing the name "Samantha".

The guard speaks first: "Katrina Miller, first punishment session."

Samantha checks through the papers on her desk and asks the prisoner to state her name and date of birth, which Katrina gives.

"Are you both staying?" Samantha asks.

"Only me," answers the guard handcuffed to Katrina.

"Okay. I don't reckon we'll be finished with her much before 6pm."

"Somebody else will have to come for you, then. I'm off at 4pm. I'll tell them to be here at 5.30pm and wait with you," states the other guard.

"Fine. This one won't know what's happening or what week it is by then."

They both laugh, and the first guard walks back along the corridor, leaving her colleague and Katrina handcuffed together.

Samantha speaks. "Go through the door on the right and take a seat in the waiting room. Someone will call you when they're ready."

The guard and her prisoner take seats in the waiting room as requested. It is a fairly large room with probably about thirty other people waiting. All, apart from Katrina, are on their own. There are roughly equal numbers of men and women. To her horror, Katrina notices that several of the people waiting are partially undressed. Three men and a couple of women are topless, and one man is completely naked. She says a silent prayer that she will not have to sit in the waiting room naked. Memories of her courtroom humiliation are still far too fresh in her memory.

Over the next half hour or so, various names are called out. Finally, a young woman calls, "Katrina Miller."

Katrina walks with the guard to where the woman is waiting and then follows her into an office with a number three on the door.

"My name is Lucy," the woman explains, "and I am a punishment assistant at this centre. I will be in charge of getting you ready for your punishments today and making sure you understand what is going to happen and when." Lucy checks Katrina's name and date of birth, and then says, "You are going to receive one-third of your caning sentence today and one-fifth of your lashes. The former equates to 250 strokes of the cane on your bare buttocks and 250 on your bare breasts. We will carry those sentences out at the same time in about half an hour or so. You will then be seen by a doctor and given treatment for your injuries, as necessary. Breasts are extremely sensitive, and you will be in tremendous pain after they have been caned. When you have been treated you will return to the waiting room. You will probably prefer to stand. We will then administer 400 lashes with the nine-tailed whip, or the 'cat' as it is sometimes called, on your bare back between your shoulders and waist. A doctor will be present for this punishment, and if he feels you are unable to continue, then the flogging will stop immediately. You will be examined and treated at the end of the whipping, as before, and then returned to the waiting room when you have recovered sufficiently. It is possible that we will brand you today, but realistically, I doubt if you will be fit enough for that. Have you ever received corporal punishment before?"

"No, I have not," replies Katrina, close to tears and scared stiff about what lies in store for her.

"It is dreadfully painful being beaten; it is meant to be, as it is punishment. Right, I need you to undress completely and put your clothes in the bag by your chair. The bag has your name on it, and you will get the clothes back at the end of the day. I doubt very much if you will want to put them on, though."

The guard unlocks the handcuffs, and for a split second, Katrina wonders if she could outrun the woman and escape. She quickly thinks better of the idea and starts to take her clothes off and bag them as instructed. Soon, she is naked, and the handcuffs are reapplied.

"Go and take a seat back in the waiting room," instructs Lucy. "I will call you when we are ready for you."

As they leave the room, the guard says quietly to Katrina, "That's it. Have a sit down whilst you still can."

It takes some time for Katrina to accept that, once again, her body is fully displayed to a number of complete strangers. Her embarrassment is not diminished by the fact that she is by no means the only person in the waiting room who is partially or completely undressed.

Time passes slowly, and Katrina's mind is full of horrible thoughts about the punishment she is to face. She decides she is most frightened of the caning on her breasts. She has always been proud of her 36C figure. Looking down at them in all their glory now, she starts to weep at the thought of what they will look like in a short while.

"I don't know why you're crying now, but I know why you'll be crying soon," the guard says, unsympathetically.

At that point, Lucy calls them, and Katrina and the guard are soon shown into punishment room five.

Katrina is strapped to a wooden desk, with her arms and legs stretched uncomfortably wide. She can hear the door open, but she cannot see who has come in.

Lucy says to the newcomer, "This is Katrina Miller. Forty-two years old and currently serving fifteen years' imprisonment. This is her first punishment session and her first ever taste of corporal punishment. Right now, she is to get 250 with the cane on her buttocks and 250 with the cane on her breasts." Lucy comes round in front of Katrina and queries, "Do you refer to them as breasts or do you use another term?"

"Tits," replies the sobbing victim.

"Okay," Lucy says brightly. "We'll try to use that term from now on."

The newcomer also walks around to Katrina's head, so the prisoner can see her. "My name is Nadia," the stranger says in a strong Indian accent. "I will be carrying out all your punishments today. I know it will be extremely unpleasant for you, but I must – by law –

deliver each stroke as hard as I can. Lucy will count each stroke. Concentrate on her and the numbers, and try to forget the pain."

Some hope of that, thinks Katrina.

"Are you staying?" Nadia asks the guard. "She's hardly in a position to run away."

"I'm staying. I've never seen breast caning before. Wouldn't miss this for anything."

"Buttocks first," decides Nadia as she moves to the back of Katrina.

Lucy remains in front of the helpless woman and gently holds her head in position.

"You ready, Lucy?" checks Nadia.

"Ready."

A few seconds of silence is followed by three separate sounds within seconds of each other. First comes the swish of the cane as it travels through the air and makes contact with Katrina's bottom. This is followed immediately by a scream from Mrs Miller.

The final sound is Lucy calling out, "One."

The same process is repeated approximately every ten seconds for roughly the next three-quarters of an hour. The only differences are the numbers being called out and the increasing desperation of Katrina's shouts, screams and pleas for mercy. Finally, the last stroke is laid on, and Lucy releases the straps. Katrina stands up unsteadily.

Lucy walks behind her to inspect the damage. "You're bleeding a bit in several places. Your bottom is bright red and quite swollen. You've certainly been well caned, but I have seen worse. I reckon it will be at least a week before you can sit or lie on that."

Katrina is given a few minutes to prepare herself for the next stage.

Far too soon, Lucy takes her over to a tall wooden frame, straps her arms and legs to it, and pulls a large strap across her stomach. "Now for your tits."

Nadia gives a brief explanation. "I am going to work in a pattern of five strokes. The first will be above your nipple on your left tit, the second below the nipple on that side, the third above your right nipple and the fourth below it. The final stroke will be across the centre of both tits. I will not deliberately aim for your nipples, but they do get hit sometimes. The stiller you can keep, the better."

The second caning of the day proceeds without problems, unless the ugly red welts and purplish-blue bruising on Katrina's breasts can be considered to be a problem.

At last, all the strokes have been given, and the nearly hysterical prisoner is released from her bonds. She stumbles and has to be supported by Lucy and the guard. They both help her to the treatment room and Nurse Penny. The guard decides to take a break, and Lucy goes off to ruin someone else's day.

Penny examines Katrina's injuries. "Your breasts aren't too bad. They've managed to avoid your nipples, which is good news. I'll put some cream on. Your arse is a different matter, though. It's bleeding quite badly in several places. That's quite a mess." The nurse pauses and gathers together the items she needs before proceeding to apply the cream.

"*Ow,*" shouts Katrina as the cream irritates her many wounds.

"Sorry," says Penny. "It stings a bit." When she finishes, the nurse says to the still-crying patient, "I'm going to get Dr Richards to look at this. How many did you get?"

"Two hundred and fifty in each area."

"Any more today?"

"Four hundred with the nine-tailed whip and branding."

"Mm, I will definitely get the doctor to examine you."

Dr Richards arrives shortly thereafter. He is a short, portly gentleman in his late forties. Katrina thinks he is far too nice to be working in a slaughterhouse like this.

After examining her, he has a whispered conversation with Penny and then speaks directly to his patient: "The good news is that I don't think you should be flogged on top of this. Although they say they only hit your back, they are using a nine-tailed whip, so you are bound to get stray strokes across your buttocks, and it is very badly cut already. The bad news is they may insist on giving you some lashes, and I imagine you will still be branded. Penny, will you put a lot more cream on her bottom? The breasts are not too bad at all, so leave them for the moment. I'll go and talk to Lucy."

*

"Come in," calls Lucy, in response to the knock on her door.

"Can you spare a minute or two?" asks Dr Richards.

"Sure. What's the matter?"

"Katrina Miller. Her buttocks are really messed up after the caning. I don't think she should have 400 lashes of the cat on top of what she's already been through."

"I didn't think her arse looked too bad. I admit she was bleeding from several places, which is unusual. Could we do some?"

"She's going to be branded today, I believe. I would feel happier if she isn't flogged at all, but she can still be branded. It's only her backside that is causing me concern."

"Well, it is her first visit. I won't be so kind next time. Okay, as soon as you feel she is over the worst of the caning, let me know, and we'll proceed to brand her."

*

Two hours later Katrina, still naked and handcuffed, is taken into a room bearing on the door the ominous words "Branding Room. Strictly No Admittance to Unauthorised Personnel." Lucy has walked to the room with Katrina and the guard. Nadia is already there, wearing protective clothing and goggles. Katrina is horrified to see that Nadia is working at an open brazier.

The room is hot and smells of smoke and fire.

The guard releases the handcuffs and says, "I will wait outside. Seeing this done once was quite enough for me."

Lucy speaks to Nadia. "She's sore front and back. Do you think we can do this with her standing up?"

"It won't be easy, but we'll try," confirms Nadia.

Lucy turns back to Katrina. "Because you are in such pain, we are doing this with you standing up instead of lying down. I am going to strap your hands behind your back and also strap your legs together. I will stand behind you holding your head still. Do not move once we are ready to start or someone will get badly hurt."

Katrina thinks, *I am already badly hurt, but that doesn't seem to bother anybody.* She decides to say nothing.

When Lucy is satisfied that the prisoner is secured tightly, she comes behind Katrina and grips her chin and the top of her head extremely tightly. "Now, whatever happens, do not move."

Nadia approaches holding a metal bar. She holds the bar against Katrina's forehead. "It's going to be a tight fit, I think," Nadia declares. She then goes over to the brazier and pushes one end of the metal into the burning coals.

At this point, Mrs Miller starts screaming and doesn't stop as Nadia takes the metal out of the fire, walks across to her and places the hot bar firmly onto Katrina's forehead. She leaves it there for a second or two before withdrawing the dreadful weapon. Immediately, there is an overpowering smell of burning flesh. The screaming stops as Katrina fades into unconsciousness. She is prevented from hitting the floor by the strapping and Lucy's quick reactions. The word "Adulteress" now shows clearly on Katrina's swollen, bright-red forehead.

Nadia picks up the phone in the room and dials internally. "Hello Dr Richards, would you come to the branding room urgently, please?" She pauses to hear his reply. "Yes, Katrina Miller. We've finished, but she's unconscious."

*

When Katrina regains consciousness, she is totally confused. She is lying in a bed, but not in her cell. After a few seconds, she realises that a guard is sitting by her bed. "Where am I?" she asks feebly.

"In hospital. You collapsed during the branding," confirms the guard.

"My head is throbbing. Have I been branded?"

"Oh yes. The whole world can see what you have been up to," the guard says, almost triumphantly. She then reaches out and presses the button to call a nurse, who arrives almost immediately.

"Good, you're awake," the nurse declares brightly. "How do you feel?"

"My head's on fire. I'm in awful pain," Katrina replies.

"Where is the pain exactly?"

"All over really, but my bottom and my tits are agony."

"Well, you have been beaten and branded today. I'll take your blood pressure and pulse. Then I'll get you some pain relief and tell the doctor that you're awake."

The guard enquires, "Is she likely to be released soon?"

"Not tonight. Her blood pressure's quite high. Tomorrow, maybe. The wounds on her buttocks seem to be infected, and we need to get that under control first. Then there's her forehead. There's so much swelling that it's impossible to tell what damage has been done, apart from the obvious."

"I'll phone the prison and tell them to get someone up here for the night shift."

After arranging the needed cover, the guard rummages through her handbag and pulls out a folding mirror. Approaching Katrina, who is lying on her side in the bed, moaning pitiably, she opens up the mirror. Katrina jerks away.

"The sooner you see what has happened, the sooner you'll get used to it. Look," the guard says, thrusting the mirror in front of the prisoner's face.

Katrina stares in disbelief at her reflection in the mirror. There is blood on her lower face, but the real horror is above her eyes. Her entire forehead is swollen, bright red and dominated by ten large letters shining out from the other damage.

She pushes the mirror away, cries uncontrollably and wishes she were dead.

*

Two days later, Katrina is returned to prison – initially, to the hospital ward and, subsequently, back to her cell to await her next visit to the punishment centre.

GOVERNMENT PRONOUNCEMENTS

February 2034: The Government announces Parliament will be dissolved one month before the general election date. The prime minister will give one interview with Sara Molan. There will be no other media interviews by the prime minister. There will be no debates with other party leaders. A limit is to be placed, with immediate effect, on the purchase of cigarettes and e-cigarettes. All citizens over the age of eighteen may buy one packet per week for their own use only.

*

Sara Molan listens to the latest pronouncements at home and buries her head a little deeper into her cushion.

CHAPTER 13

DUGG

FEBRUARY 2034

Dugg Nicholson is twenty-four years old and has over fifty convictions, mostly for shoplifting. An alcoholic, he mostly steals drink and, occasionally, food. He has been out of prison for less than twenty-four hours before he is caught trying to walk out of a supermarket with two bottles of whisky. Dugg is a nuisance, but he is never violent, and waits quite calmly and patiently with the store detective for the police to arrive.

He is taken to the police station, where he is charged, given a cell for the night and awaits his appearance in court the next day.

*

Dugg knows the court procedures better than most of the magistrates, and he has not needed or used a solicitor for years. The three magistrates enter the courtroom and take their places. The court clerk reads out the charge of attempting to steal two bottles of whisky and asks Dugg whether he pleads guilty or not guilty.

He answers, "Guilty."

The prosecutor, Ms Williamson, rises. "This defendant is no stranger to this court. In fact, he has fifty-three previous convictions. Mr Nicholson was only released from incarceration on the day prior to this latest offence. There is an unbreakable pattern going back several years. The defendant is caught stealing, appears in court, pleads guilty and is sent to prison. He is then released back into the real world, and the same chain of events reoccurs, usually within days of him regaining his freedom. The prison sentences are getting longer, but there is no change whatsoever in Mr Nicholson's behaviour."

"Is alcohol the reason for this repeated offending?" one of the magistrates asks Ms Williamson.

"It is the main reason, definitely. The defendant is of no fixed address, and on occasion, has stolen items such as blankets and food in order to improve his living conditions. Mainly, though, it is alcohol – particularly bottles of whisky – that he targets," she explains.

"Is the accused being released from prison with no accommodation or money?"

"Maybe he has in the past, but this time, a place has been found for him at a local hostel. Mr Nicholson has chosen to sleep on the street rather than take up this place."

The magistrate turns towards the dock. "Why on earth would you pass up a chance of a warm bed with meals provided?"

"They're all crazy in those places. They'd stick a knife in your back as soon as look at you," answers Dugg.

"And not being able to drink in the hostel has nothing to do with it, of course?"

"Well, that as well."

The magistrates confer, and then the leader of the bench addresses the court clerk: "Do we have any options other than sending the defendant to prison yet again?"

"All community-based punishments have been abolished under the present government. You do have the option of corporal punishment. To the best of my knowledge, it has never been used as a sentence for shoplifting, but in theory, it can be used for any crime," responds the clerk.

Dugg becomes quite agitated in the dock at this suggestion. "No way. There's no way you're hitting me for stealing booze. That's not on."

"Looks like we've struck a nerve there, Mr Nicholson," the magistrate observes. "You have to make some kind of effort here. We keep sending you to prison, and you come out and go straight back to stealing. If jail does not work for you, then we are entitled to try something else."

"Send me back inside for as long as you like, but I beg you, no beatings. I've seen lads come back after a caning. They can barely walk and can't sit down. Even real tough lads are crying hours afterwards. That is not happening to me."

The magistrates confer again, and the leader questions the court clerk once more: "What is the maximum prison sentence we can impose for this offence?"

"There is no limit nowadays," the clerk states. "The longest sentence the defendant has been given is six months, but he only served three months. The term just completed was for five months."

After further conferring, the chief magistrate addresses Dugg once more: "I have never been involved in a decision like this, Mr Nicholson. We have decided to give you a choice. You can go to prison for twelve months, or you can go to prison for six months and also receive 200 strokes of the cane on your bare buttocks. The choice is entirely yours."

Ms Williamson stands up. "This is most improper. It is up to you to make a decision, not to get the defendant to do your job for you."

"*No, no. That is fine by me,*" shouts out Dugg, agitated again. "I am more than happy to choose. I want the twelve months and no beating."

"That seems a perfectly free choice to me, Ms Williamson. Clerk of the Court, do you have any objections or legal impediments?" questions the magistrate.

"There is nothing I can find to stop you, legally speaking. We can rely on the fact that the defendant has expressed his preference very clearly, so I am happy for you to proceed."

"Mr Nicholson, I promise you that if you come out of jail in twelve months' time and reoffend, your next sentence will include caning. You need to break this vicious circle, and between us, we might just have found a way to do it. The decision of this court is that you are sentenced to a term of imprisonment not exceeding twelve months."

Grinning madly, Dugg replies, "Thank you. I will never steal again."

*

Despite being the prosecutor, Ms Williamson visits Dugg before he is transported to prison, so as to advise him that the magistrates should not have acted in that way, and therefore he has a case to appeal against the sentence. He politely but firmly tells her to go away.

*

Sara is preparing for a studio interview with political editor Richard Newbury about the forthcoming general election. Her phone beeps, and she finds another message from Bob counting down to their interview. She deletes it, grabs her notes and heads for the studio thinking, *I much preferred it when he sent flowers and chocolates.*

She starts the interview by introducing Richard and then asks him about the latest opinion poll on the forthcoming general election.

He explains, "This programme has commissioned a poll asking people who they intend to vote for and their rating of the party leaders. The result is that 40% say they will vote Labour, 35% Conservative, 10% Common Sense and 9% Liberal. As far as leadership is concerned, Sir Keir Starmer tops the poll with 47%, Michael Gove has 38% and Bob Godwin has 3%. The Liberals, of course, have yet to announce who will lead them into the vote."

"Do we have any manifestos yet?"

"No, not yet. It is still over two months to the general election. Sir Keir Starmer has issued a statement saying that if he becomes prime minister, he will immediately repeal the entire Justice Act 2029. This would abolish the death penalty, ban all corporal punishment, and cancel all legislation relating to people's marital and sexual choices. That would put us back to the position immediately before the 2029 general election when same-sex couples could live together and marry, and mixed-sex couples had no restrictions whatsoever on their private activities. The Conservatives are expected to say more or less the same thing on this matter. Both opposition parties have voted against every clause of the Justice Act, so it would be a great shock if any of that legislation survives a change of government."

"What are the chances of another Common Sense government?"

"Going by the opinion polls, not great. However, they were not predicted to do particularly well five years ago, but they gained a landslide win. Bob Godwin's personal rating is incredibly low. Common Sense have not issued their manifesto yet. The prime minister is due to be interviewed in early April by you, Sara. I imagine they will wait until then to launch the manifesto on the back of that interview and hope that Bob Godwin can win over some undecided voters with a sparkling performance. No pressure then, Sara."

"I believe there is some news about my former colleague David McDougall."

"Just to remind viewers, David fronted Common Sense's general election drive five years ago, but he has been sitting as an independent MP for most of this Parliament. He has announced in the last hour that he has formed a new political party called Liberation. He will be standing under that party's banner at the general election. There are no policy announcements yet, but I would suggest he, too, will want to reverse many of the changes originated by Common Sense. David has called on those Common Sense MPs who feel that party is not the right platform for them any more to join his party now and stand as Liberation candidates."

"Is that likely to happen?"

"No Common Sense MP has ever voted against or abstained on a government bill or motion. Privately, though, some are worried about the direction of the party recently. Regulations on vegetarianism, chocolate and cigarettes coupled with the draconian punishments being meted out daily concern many. Some may be tempted to jump ship and regroup under a different name."

"And a different, more moderate leader?"

"Exactly."

"Coming back to the polls, why do you think the opposition parties are doing so well at the moment? What is it they are doing that the Government isn't?"

"Quite frankly, it is what the Government *is* doing that is affecting the polls. They were elected five years ago to cut crime, and they have done that spectacularly if you just judge based on crime rates. However, many voters massively dislike the methods used to achieve the reduction. The mood in the country seems to be for a more moderate approach. It could be that the prime minister will take a less sadistic approach in his interview and the party's manifesto. If he does, there could yet be a surge in support for Common Sense. Stranger things have happened in politics."

"Richard, do you think the economy will be an important element in this general election?"

"It should be. The economy is underperforming. The Covid-19 pandemic cost thousands of billions of pounds, which is going to have a detrimental effect on virtually every country in the world for decades to come. These last five years have seen some economies start on the long road to recovery. We are, at best, exactly where we were five years ago. The latest figures are due next week, so it will be interesting to see whether they are showing any growth."

"Why are we struggling?"

"The Government, in its wisdom, decided to cancel the trade deal with the EU and switch to a new arrangement with the USA. I think it is fair to say that this new deal is not currently living up to expectations."

"What other subjects will play a part in electors' minds in the run up to general election day?"

"The NHS [National Health Service] is always a favourite topic. It is gradually recovering from the pandemic. Recruitment has been hit badly, though, by the ban on immigration, and many health workers have decided to return to their native countries for different reasons, including Covid-19. Climate change is another regular general election topic. The Conservatives under Boris Johnson did some good work in this area, but there has been no interest from the present government. The Green Party lost their sole MP at the last general election, but they will be hoping to regain ground this time so they can keep climate change and the environment in the public eye. The final subject I would mention is a slightly unusual one: communications. The recent polls have shown that the general public detest Bob Godwin's policy of issuing proclamations when he wishes people to be aware of a new law or a change in policy. Also, the lack of interviews and press conferences annoys many voters. I have no doubt that you are aware you are the only person to interview Bob Godwin in his whole term of office."

"I'm honoured," responds Sara, with far less sincerity than she had hoped to impart.

"I do think the party that can get its message across the best will have a good chance of winning."

"Are we going to see battle buses and soapboxes this time round?"

"I doubt it. This general election is most likely to be won and lost on the internet. We are going to see much greater usage of social media websites and pop-up messages than ever before."

"Ignore anything in Russian would be my advice."

"I think the sheer volume is going to overwhelm even the most fanatical follower of politics. Coronavirus may have finally left us, but many people are still wary, so the traditional door-to-door canvassing is bound to be reduced in favour of the internet, mailshots and emails. One thing we will definitely not be dealing with this year is leaders' debates. Bob Godwin has the final word on this, and he is adamant that he will not take part in any debates at all. Without him, the TV companies have decided not to stage any this time around."

"Thank you, Richard. It looks as if we could be in for a very exciting and different general election campaign in the coming months. That concludes our show for today. Goodbye."

CHAPTER 14

IRINA

MARCH 2034

Although much of Westminster is affected by break-up fever with the general election just two months away, elsewhere, the day-to-day work of overcoming crime continues. In Plymouth, undercover officers are arranging an operation to investigate a suspected brothel.

A detective starts the sting by phoning a number known to be associated with the premises. He arranges an appointment with Daria at 9pm in the name of Mike West.

At the agreed time, a plain-clothes officer arrives at the property and rings the bell. After giving his name, he is buzzed in and finds himself in a wide corridor. A middle-aged woman sits behind a desk. Mike approaches her and explains he has an appointment with Daria. The woman doesn't answer, but she points to a row of plastic chairs lined up against the right-hand wall. Mike takes a seat and examines his surroundings, not that there is much to see. A few yards further down the corridor is a door marked "Private" and the corridor continues beyond that. There seem to be a number of rooms on both sides of the passageway.

After a few minutes, a young, blonde woman comes through the "Private" door. She is tall, slim and unquestionably extremely good-looking. She also has an exceptional figure and is wearing only a bikini. She speaks in a strong East European accent: "I Daria. You Mike?"

"Yes, I am," replies Mike, thinking how much he loves this job.

"Come through." Daria turns and goes back through the door, followed by Mike.

They enter the second room on the right-hand side.

"What would you like?" she enquires.

"What's on offer?" Mike counters.

"Hand relief. Blow job. Sex. All with a condom. Cash up front."

Mike pulls out his wallet and takes out several £20 notes. "How much just to talk for a few minutes first? This is my first time doing anything like this."

Daria grabs all the money and tucks it inside her bikini top. "Sit on the bed."

Mike does as he is told, and she pulls a chair up close to him. Very close, in fact.

She moves her face near to his and starts kissing his lips. When he withdraws slightly, she says, "Kissing, yes? Better than talking." One of her hands starts wandering down his body.

Mike edges away from her and pulls his police walkie-talkie out of his shirt pocket. "*Now. Now. Now,*" he shouts.

Daria moves backwards, but Mike grabs her.

"You're under arrest on suspicion of prostitution," he declares.

"No understand," comes the reply.

Mike laughs. "You understand just fine." He then cautions her and holds on to her until other officers enter the room. "How many?"

A female police officer answers, "The receptionist, two other girls and two customers. Hard at it, shall we say. Both of them."

"Will you do something before I leave you with her? Would you get our bait money back? Lovely Daria here put it down her bikini top as soon as she got her hands on it. I'll turn away."

"Hand it over," demands the female officer.

Daria reaches inside her top and takes out the money from deep inside her ample cleavage.

"All right, Mike, you can look now. Here's £120. That right?"

"No, there should be one more."

"Hand it over now or I'll make you take the bikini off," the female officer says to Daria.

Daria frowns, but she retrieves the money and puts it in the officer's hand somewhat annoyedly.

"I've arrested her and cautioned her, so she is all yours," Mike says, as he leaves the room.

The female officer asks Daria where her clothes are and stays with her whilst she puts on jeans and a vest top. The officer takes her bag and looks through it, finding a credit card and Ukrainian passport. They are both in the name of Irina Katowinicz, age twenty-two, with an address in Kiev. "Who's Daria, then?"

"My professional name."

*

At Plymouth police station, Irina is interviewed by DS John Attaway and DC Fiona Edwards. DS Attaway is in his late forties. He is a very experienced officer who has seen and done it all. He would love to be promoted, but is moody, has difficulties with authority and is too much one of the boys to stand much chance of advancement nowadays. DC Edwards is twenty-three years old and very single. She has a degree in criminology and her father is a career officer, who is currently serving as an inspector based at headquarters in Exeter.

"Irina, do you want a translator?" DC Edwards enquires.

"No. I speak good and understand better," she confirms.

"How long have you been in this country?" asks DS Attaway.

"Two months," Irina replies sulkily.

"How did you come to this country?"

"Lady bring six of us from Kyiv on Aeroflot. I and one other in Plymouth."

"Do you know this lady's name?"

"No."

"How much did you pay?"

"Nothing to come. I pay off travel from my work."

"Do you keep some of the money you earn or do the owners of the brothel take it all?"

"They take one-fifth of all I earn for food and bed, and one-fifth towards my airfare. I get the rest."

"Plus whatever you can slip down your bikini top," says DC Edwards.

Irina shrugs. "A girl has to live. The less clothes cover, the more they cost."

"What are the names of the owners of the brothel?" DS Attaway continues.

"I say no more. Nothing. Just deport me now."

"It's not as easy as that. You are under arrest and you will appear in court tomorrow morning. If you plead guilty, you will probably be sentenced then. If you plead not guilty, you will be sent to prison until your trial. You will only be sent back to Ukraine when you have served your sentence."

"Just take me to a plane. I have money on card. I go. Not come back here."

"No. It does not work like that now."

"How will I be punished? I pay fine easy."

DC Edwards replies, "You will be imprisoned, beaten, branded and deported."

Irina looks shocked. "No. Deport me first, please. Forget the rest."

"This country takes a tough line on prostitution. Sentences are tough to deter people like you from sneaking into the country to become sex workers," explains DS Attaway. "What work did you do in Kiev?"

"Some modelling, but mostly as escort and prostitute."

"Since when?"

"Since I was fifteen."

"Do you have a boyfriend or relative in this country?"

"No. Relatives in Kyiv, but they lock door on me at fifteen. Boyfriend in Kyiv. My how do you say? Pump… pomp…"

"Pimp," the two officers say together.

"Pimp. He arranges my customers. I leave Ukraine to get away from him, but I take my chances rather than be beaten."

"Not your choice, Irina. Let's find you a cell for the night," concludes DS Attaway.

*

The next morning, Irina appears in court and pleads guilty to prostitution. She asks to be sentenced immediately and also asks to be deported to Ukraine instead of being punished.

Judge Andrews replies, "I am happy to sentence you right now. You will be deported at the end of your sentence and not before. You committed a crime here and you will be punished here."

"Please. I go home now. No come back," she offers.

"Sorry, no. The present government of this country has decided that it wishes to stamp out the evil of prostitution once and for all. I have minimum punishments I must impose on everyone guilty of this heinous crime—"

Irina interrupts: "'Heinous', I no understand."

"Terrible crime." The judge continues, "You have entered this country under false pretences, posing as a student, and have worked as a prostitute ever since your arrival in Plymouth. You were caught red-handed by an undercover police officer; you offered him a menu of sex acts and had no hesitation in taking money from him in return for sexual activity. This case is well beyond the minimum punishment for prostitution, so I have no choice but to impose a punishment well beyond the minimum required by the law. Irina Katowinicz, you are sentenced to a term of imprisonment not exceeding five years. In addition, you will receive a total of 1,000 strokes of the cane on your bare buttocks and 1,000 strokes of the nine-tailed whip on your bare back. You will be branded on your forehead as a prostitute and deported to Ukraine at the end of your prison sentence."

"What the fuck? You mad. You crazy. You not fuckin' whipping me."

"Take her away," says Judge Andrews sternly. "Before I punish her for contempt of court as well."

It takes three guards to bundle Irina out of the dock successfully and down the steps to the cells.

*

Two days later, DS Attaway and DC Edwards are called into Detective Chief Inspector (DCI) Pitman's office.

He explains, "I've had an interesting phone call from Exeter women's prison. Do you remember that Ukrainian tom you interviewed a few days ago? She's been to see the governor today, saying she has important information and she wants to do a deal."

"I can guess what she wants, but do we have any idea what she is offering?" asks DS Attaway.

"The governor thinks it could be big. I want you to go up there and see what this is all about. Don't promise anything, but get as much out of her as possible. Keep me informed."

"Does it have to be us? We're up to our eyes in the flasher case."

"The lady says she will speak to nobody but the two of you. The prison is expecting you at 2pm."

*

DC Edwards drives them up to Exeter. Throughout the journey, DS Attaway moans about his workload and what a complete waste of time this is. On arrival, they pass through security and are shown into a deserted visitors' room.

A few minutes later, Irina is brought into the room, wearing a prison uniform of white blouse and grey tracksuit bottoms. She still looks remarkably beautiful despite a lack of make-up.

"What do you want?" DS Attaway demands irritably.

"To do deal," she states.

"And what do you want from us?"

"Deportation back to Cracow, Poland, before these bastards start ruining my beauty for ever."

"Not a chance, darling. Come on. Let's go," says DS Attaway, rising from his chair.

"Hang on, Sarge. I'm curious even if you aren't," DC Edwards intervenes.

"You have a Ukrainian passport, but now you want to go back to Poland?" questions Attaway.

"I have Ukrainian passport, but I am Polish citizen. If you listen to me, you will understand why I cannot return to Kiev now," Irina declares.

"Go on," urges DC Edwards.

"My boyfriend in Kyiv gets tired of me and sells me to traffickers to work in brothel overseas so he can fuck fourteen-year-old," she explains. "I spend three weeks working in brothel in Kiev, then I am taken to airport and flown to London with five other girls. Then driven to

Plymouth, where I work for two months in brothel where your Mike catch me. I clever girl. I remember well. I can tell you names of people owning brothel in Kyiv. I tell you name of woman who flies with us and man who meets us in London. I also know famous people who come to brothel in Plymouth. MP, high policeman, judge. All I ask in return is no prison, no beating and no branding. I stay to sign statement and then go back to Cracow."

DS Attaway has sat down again and is interested now. "Why should we trust you? Every time you open your mouth it is a different story."

"I scared in police station and scared in court. I trust you, but nobody else," Irina tells them.

"We can't deal with this on our own. If you are telling the truth, then we will need help from colleagues to act on all this," concludes DS Attaway.

DC Edwards tries to calm the girl. "We can move you from here to somewhere safe. Why were you scared at the police station?"

"I see one of the owners of brothel." Irina looks very worried at this.

"Do you know his name?" DC Edwards questions.

"Pitman," states Irina.

"Shit!" exclaims Attaway.

DC Edwards continues probing: "Why were you scared in court?"

Irina pauses before answering. "I see regular client. He not know me. He has special girl – same one every time. He send me here and want to destroy my body."

"Are you saying Judge Andrews is mixed up in this?" DC Edwards looks incredulous at this.

"Yes." Irina nods in confirmation.

"This makes no sense at all," DS Attaway says quietly to DC Edwards. "Pitman would have known all about the raid. He would have warned them to shut, surely?"

"He didn't know though, did he? He's been away at the Police Federation conference the whole week whilst it was being planned. His first shift back was the night shift on the day of the raid," clarifies DC Edwards.

"Are you sure?"

"Superintendent Carter okayed the raid. I remember Mike telling me he'd been put through the third degree by him."

"Why has DCI Pitman sent us up here when he must suspect what she is going to tell us?"

"He knows Irina as Daria. He thinks he is safe because he has never been to that brothel with an Irina there." DC Edwards addresses her next question to Irina. "You saw Pitman at the police station. Did he see you?"

"No. He was sideways to me, talking to another officer. I stood behind another girl so he would not see me. I need your help to prove this. They took my bag when I came here. I have photographs of Pitman and Andrews taken secretly in the brothel. Get me my bag and scissors. I show you," she offers.

"I can see my pension slipping away here," sighs DS Attaway. "Who the hell can we trust?"

"The governor – a good man," answers Irina.

"We can trust my father," DC Edwards suggests.

"Is he high up enough for this?" queries DS Attaway.

"No, but he works at headquarters. He should know who *is* high up enough and can be trusted."

"Right. We need a plan. I will go and speak to the governor. I'll get another officer in here with you whilst I'm gone. Not a word from either of you. We trust no one. Understand? I'll try to get the bag, and if there is proof, then you speak to your father. He can explain this to someone at headquarters, and if it all works out, we'll take Irina there to tell her story to the right people."

"Sounds so simple when you put it like that."

"If you are lying," DS Attaway tells Irina firmly. "I will personally flog and brand you before I go back to Plymouth. Understand?"

"I tell truth. I really scared. Too scared to lie now," she confirms.

*

Irina and Fiona sit in silence with a middle-aged, female prison officer for an uncomfortably long time. Eventually, DS Attaway returns, but he is not alone. The governor enters behind him, carrying a large bag and two pairs of scissors of noticeably different sizes. The prison officer departs.

Irina says, "I need small scissors. This delicate work."

She takes the bag and rummages through it before bringing out a large mirror. She takes the scissors and very carefully creates a small gap in the felt backing of the mirror. Slowly, she starts to peel away the backing. As she does so, something is revealed to be tucked in between the backing and the mirror. Once she has peeled away enough of the backing, Irina pulls out two photographs. One shows DCI Pitman and two other men talking in a corridor with a number of rooms along the hallway, each bearing a number on the door. The other photograph shows Judge Andrews in the same corridor with a naked, young brunette.

"There," declares Irina triumphantly.

"So much for bag searches," DC Edwards comments ruefully.

"One more concealment to add to the list," responds the governor.

"This doesn't prove anything. It could have been taken anywhere," interjects DS Attaway.

"We didn't see the place, but we know someone who did and is totally trustworthy," suggests DC Edwards.

"Mike West. I'll ring him." DS Attaway takes out his mobile phone and makes the call. "Hello Mike, it's John Attaway. Where are you?"

"At home, trying to enjoy a rare day off," Mike replies.

"Good, I need your help. Would you describe the brothel premises you raided earlier in the week?"

"Why? What's going on?"

"I can't say, and don't tell anyone I've contacted you. Okay?"

"I rang a bell and then spoke to a woman who buzzed me in. I was in a corridor, which was painted white. Everything was painted white. At the end of the corridor was a desk and a woman sitting behind it. There were some plastic chairs on the right-hand side. Daria came out of a door marked 'Private', and we went back through it together into a continuation of the corridor. There were about six rooms each side, with numbers on the doors. We went into room two. The corridor and the room were painted white, like a bloody hospital."

"Mike, what colour was the number two on the door?"

"Very unusual. There were two colours: black at the top and white at the bottom."

"Thanks, Mike. Not a word, remember." DS Attaway hangs up the call and turns to the governor. "These photos could be any brothel or any building, but there is one unusual feature: the door numbers are two tone – black and white. There can't be too many places with those on the doors. I can't believe I'm saying this, but it looks like she's telling the truth. I would like to formally request the temporary release of the prisoner Irina Katowinicz into my custody for the purpose of transporting her to police headquarters."

"You'll have to sign for her," states the governor.

"Time to ring your father," suggests DS Attaway to DC Edwards.

Half an hour later, Inspector Edwards greets the trio at the police headquarters. DC Edwards is handcuffed to Irina, so when her father pulls her to one side to talk to her privately, the prisoner comes too.

"Are you positive about this?" the inspector asks his daughter. "Attaway will take any opportunity to tackle authority. This could be a career-ender."

"DS Attaway is a good cop. We've verified as much as we can. We have photographs and another officer has given us a description of the brothel which matches the photographs. And we have a witness willing to give a full statement." DC Edwards nods at the prisoner.

"I good girl. I tell truth," contributes Irina.

"You'd better pray she is. This is going to stir up a right can of worms." Raising his voice, Inspector Edwards addresses all three of the group. "I'm going to take you through to see the chief constable. You address him as 'sir', and answer his questions simply and truthfully. He hates wafflers and liars."

"What is his name?" asks Irina, looking thoughtful.

"Brian Cook," replies Inspector Edwards.

"Ring any bells?" Fiona asks Irina, praying silently for a negative answer.

"No," confirms Irina.

"Thank God for that." DS Attaway is visibly relieved.

Inspector Edwards leads them through a maze of corridors until they come to a door marked "Chief

Constable Brian Cook".

The inspector knocks, and a shout of, "*Come in*," is the response.

The office is huge, and a well-built man in his fifties with jet-black hair sits at a desk at the far end. The quartet walk up to the desk, with Irina still handcuffed to Fiona Edwards. The inspector addresses the chief constable. "Sir, these are DS John Attaway, DC Fiona Edwards and a convicted prostitute named Irina Katowinicz, who claims she has important information about a judge and a DCI on this force."

"Thank you, Inspector. If you could leave us now, please," replies the chief constable. "A good man; I hope you are proud of him." Chief Constable Cook directs this remark at DC Edwards.

"Yes, I am sir. Very proud," says DC Edwards.

For the next few minutes, Irina tells her story again, and then DS Attaway shows Chief Constable Cook the photographs.

"How have you verified these?" the chief constable enquires.

"I spoke to the officer who posed as a client and saw the inside of the premises," DS Attaway explains.

"He only want talk. Must be gay," Irina grumbles irritably, then quickly adds, "Sir."

"What do you want from us?" Chief Constable Cook queries.

"Cancel conviction. No punishment. Plane to Cracow. Sir."

"And what do I get?"

"All names. Statement from me on the Bible. The photographs."

"I take it you do not want to stay around for a trial?"

"No. I stay in Cracow. No Plymouth. No Kyiv. Not safe for Irina. Sir."

"I want to film you reading your statement and swearing on the Bible. I want that done here. Inspector Edwards will interview you. Then I will decide what to do next."

At this point, a knock comes on the door and Inspector Edwards enters. "I am sorry to interrupt, sir, but we have a problem. The prison governor has just phoned. DCI Pitman has rung him, wanting to know where his officers are and why they haven't reported in."

"What did he say?" asks the chief constable.

"Nothing. He said he would look into it and ring back."

"Tell him to say there has been a problem. The prisoner kicked off when she was told the officers weren't interested in what she had to say. Tell him his officers were injured slightly and are being treated. They will be heading home once they have recovered. Will someone release the prisoner, please? Inspector, will you take Irina and get her statement. When she has signed it, I want her filmed swearing on a Bible and reading it aloud in full. And for God's sake, don't let her escape. I'm lying to a DCI. We're all out on a limb here."

Irina responds, "No film in these clothes. I want glamorous. Not enough to jail me, whip me and brand me. Now set me up for attack police officers."

The chief constable replies, "Actually, she's right. I don't want her in prison uniform. Any good defence lawyer will use it against us. DC Edwards go with them and stay in the room with her when she changes. I want respectable, not glamorous."

"I think, sir, that respectable might be a bit difficult with the wardrobe she has here. I think it is a choice between a bikini or jeans and vest top," DC Edwards chips in.

"Do what you can. DS Attaway, stay here please. The rest of you come back here when you are done," commands the chief constable.

When the others have left the room, Chief Constable Cook addresses the DS. "What do you make of all this?"

"I think it is a huge success for the Government's policy on harsh sentencing. She is terrified of being branded and flogged. More terrified than she is of the people she is naming. She has lied to us about her name, her nationality and about the information she is now offering. She is very different today than before she was sentenced. She is genuinely afraid now, and I consider she is telling the truth," DS Attaway states.

"DCI Pitman is suspicious. I don't think what the governor says will hold him for very long. Who is the senior officer on duty at Plymouth today?"

"Superintendent Carter. He authorised the raid in the first place, so it is highly unlikely he is involved in any of this."

"Right. I will ring him. I think we need to arrest DCI Pitman right now, before he becomes more suspicious."

He goes on to tell DS Attaway to stay as a witness whilst he rings Superintendent Carter. The conversation is terse, but the chief constable gets his own way.

A few minutes later, the phone rings. After a brief conversation, Cook turns to the DS and says, "DCI Pitman is under arrest. He's very unhappy and refusing to talk without consulting his Police Federation representative. At least he has his own office, so it stays relatively secret."

"What about Judge Andrews?" asks DS Attaway.

"We'll draw up a list of suspects and form a team, led by you, to get to the bottom of this. Send the girl back to Poland when you are absolutely sure you've got every minor detail you need from her. We will not get her back under any circumstances; I can assure you of that."

"Do you have the authority to cancel her conviction?"

"Actually, I do. The infamous Justice Act 2029, which I am sure you know backwards, gives me the power to overturn court decisions if there is judicial corruption. I doubt if the powers have ever been used, and I am sure our prime minister would not be happy with the Act leading to a convicted prostitute getting away without a mark on her."

"I can rough her up on the way to the airport, sir?"

"Don't tempt me. These days, it is perfectly all right for a punishment centre officer to scar someone for life, but heaven help us if we so much as break one of her fingernails."

At that point, there is a knock on the door, and DC Edwards and Irina enter, still handcuffed together. Irina is now wearing jeans and a vest top, last seen when initially interviewed at Plymouth police station. Inspector Edwards follows them in and hands several pieces of paper to the chief constable. The inspector then sets up a DVD player and awaits further instruction.

Chief Constable Cook reads the papers carefully and then hands them on to DS Attaway. "Is this the truth?" he asks Irina.

"It is, sir," she replies. "I go now?"

"No, you do not go now. I have asked DS Attaway to form a team of officers to follow up on your information. Only when he is satisfied that you are not sending him off on a wild goose chase will you be allowed to leave."

Irina looks confused. "How long catch these geese?"

DS Attaway explains, "We have suspects in Ukraine, Poland and here, so it will take a few days, maybe a week. Sir, is it all right if I ask DC Edwards to join the team?"

"Yes, of course. It is thanks to the good work of both of you that we are in this position. Inspector Edwards, I would like you to act as overseeing officer on this," orders the chief constable.

"Certainly, sir," agrees Inspector Edwards.

Irina is next to speak. "Well done. Everybody get something but me. No go home. I no go back to prison. Sir."

"What are we going to do with her, sir?" asks Attaway, as all eyes turn to DC Edwards.

"No. No, you must be joking," declares DC Edwards.

*

It is midnight by the time Fiona and Irina, no longer joined at the wrist, arrive at the police officer's house in Plympton.

"What do you want to eat or drink, Irina?" Fiona queries.

"No eat. Large vodka," demands Irina.

"I meant tea or coffee."

"Coffee, black. I want look in your wardrobe."

"Go ahead. My room's the one straight in front of you when you go up the stairs."

Once the kettle has boiled and she has made their drinks, Fiona carries them upstairs. Her bedroom looks as if a bomb has hit it. Shoes, clothes and jewellery are scattered everywhere. "What are you looking for?"

"Your uniform is horrible, but you look better in it than anything here: tracksuits, trainers, flat shoes, great-grandma's jewellery and, worst of all, a single bed. You are young, sexy, attractive. Why you dress like fifty-year-old?"

"You don't understand, Irina. For the last five years, all women have been forbidden to have sex other than with their husband. No sex before marriage, no same-gender sex – nothing."

"Are you gay?"

"No. Just celibate."

"No understand."

"It means I'm not getting any."

"And you never will with clothes like this. Tomorrow, we go shopping. Buy sexy clothes."

"Irina, I am a policewoman and a single person. I do not do sexy. I am not allowed to do sexy. Nobody of my age does sexy. Nobody of my age does sex. If we do, at best, we lose our jobs and freedom. At worst, we lose the skin from our backs, bottoms and breasts."

"How many lovers have you had?"

"That's personal."

"Which means none. How many boyfriends?"

"A couple, but nothing long lasting. It is hard. I have lived in four different places in the last two years. As soon as I get settled somewhere, I am transferred. And even you would find it harder to pull if you had to tell men you were a police officer."

It takes Fiona nearly an hour to sort out the chaos Hurricane Irina has brought to her bedroom.

*

The police operation progresses well. Judge Andrews is arrested and charged with soliciting prostitution. Police forces in Poland and Ukraine move quickly to arrest the people named in Irina's statement, ultimately resulting in the dismantling of an international prostitution ring. Chief Constable Cook acts to replace DCI Pitman, and of course, this one promotion creates a vacancy. By the time it is decided to release Irina, her fellow travellers on the way to the airport are Detective Inspector (DI) John Attaway and DS Fiona Edwards.

"Congratulations on your promotions," says Irina.

"And congratulations to you on avoiding prison, caning, flogging and branding. Plus, you get a free plane ticket out of here. I'm surprised we aren't filling your bag with euros," DI Attaway replies.

"Take no notice," comments DS Edwards. "He's always like this first thing in the morning. He loves you, really. What are your plans then, Irina?"

"Stay away from Kyiv. Perhaps new name. Find rich, good-looking man who not pomp," she confirms.

"*Pimp!*" the police officers shout in unison.

"If not, prostitute."

"Irina, you are worth more than that. You are a resourceful, intelligent woman, albeit with lousy taste in clothes. You do not have to demean yourself to men for money," responds Fiona.

"You are right. I run brothel, not work in it." Irina looks thoughtful as she leaves them.

As they watch her go through the departure gate, turning heads in a purple mini skirt and a bright-red crop top, DS Edwards says, "I shall miss her. It is going to seem so quiet at home tonight. Perhaps we shall see her again."

"I hope not," declares DI Attaway.

"That's a bit unkind, seeing as she got you a promotion you couldn't quite achieve on your own."

"Oh, come on! All you've done is moan about her ever since she moved in with you."

"That is true, but her heart is in the right place. She bought me something online last night to remember her by."

"Please tell me it is a vest top."

"Behave yourself. It is an illustrated copy of *The Kama Sutra*."

"All you need now is a man and a wedding ring."

"Wrong again. All I need now is a man and a change of government."

CHAPTER 15

SARA

APRIL 2034

Sara Molan's show on Monday, 3rd April 2034 appears to the audience watching at home to be no different to any other day. The same topical guests, and the same acerbic questioning and speculation about the general election just four weeks and three days away. Sara, however, is struggling to concentrate as her mind is filled with just one thing: her interview at 8pm with Prime Minister Bob Godwin.

Straight after the programme, she attends a meeting with William Marshall to discuss in detail the arrangements for what Sara is openly calling "the interview from hell."

"Sara, have you received the questions yet?" he asks.

"No. I imagine he is going to spring them on me when I arrive," Sara speculates. "I do know that we are filming in one of the rooms in his private accommodation in 11 Downing Street. There will be two fixed cameras, but no one operating them. One will be fixed on me and one on Bob Godwin. I've been practising my blank expression for days, but no one's noticed. The prime minister's people will edit the tape overnight and get it to you to show instead of the programme tomorrow."

"Are you coming into the studio to watch it?"

"Definitely not. I shall be in bed recovering from spending the evening with the world's most obnoxious man."

"For God's sake, don't tell him that. You're not the only one with something to lose here, Sara."

"I know the rules. Only his questions to be asked, no comments, no interruptions and no criticism. Why on earth he wants to do this with a sarcastic, argumentative presenter when he could have Grandma Horton is beyond me."

"He wants to tame you, so the whole country can see what a dominant personality he has. Just let the opponent win this once. With a bit of luck, he'll be out of our hair in a month's time."

"I need you to do something for me. I have got to be there at 8pm, so we'll probably start taping about 8.30pm. I'm a professional even if he isn't, so we'll be finished by 9.30pm or thereabouts. Then I think there is food being laid on. So, I want you to ring my mobile around 10pm. You don't have to say anything at all. I'll do the talking and tell Bob I have to go. My flat is flooded or something. I won't feel safe until I'm back in my own place with the door firmly locked."

"You're being paranoid. You're going to Downing Street, not some dogging site. Even Bob Godwin isn't going to come on heavy in the prime minister's residence."

"Perhaps you are right, but just don't forget to make that call."

Sara then heads for home and a chance to rest for a few hours before the second part of her working day.

*

She has barely got inside the door when her mobile buzzes. She checks it and discovers a new message from Bob: "Sara, I've been thinking. Wear a really short skirt and the thinnest blouse you own. Black tights will look good. Actually, black stockings will look even better. Don't forget you're staying the night."

"*Sod you,*" she yells at the walls before bursting into tears.

Somehow, she manages to snatch an hour's sleep before waking just after 5pm.

Against her better judgement, Sara searches through her wardrobe and finds two skirts that finish above her knees. She rejects the shorter of the two and settles on a slightly more modest black mini. Tights are no problem. She mutters to herself. "Even if I had any stockings, I wouldn't wear them for that pervert." Next, she selects a white blouse that is thick enough to hide her breasts from public scrutiny, even without a bra. Sara looks at herself in the mirror and thinks. "I look like a bloody schoolgirl." She spends too long looking for alternatives, but cannot find anything better.

Her next job is to order a cab for 7.30pm and then she does her hair and make-up before checking her phone: "Sara. I'm sending my chauffeur to collect you at 7.30pm."

She mutters, "Damn," to herself and cancels the taxi.

The clock now says 7.15pm. She checks her emails, spends several minutes redoing her hair and checking her make-up, and then grabs her coat and bag, putting her phone in a pocket. She exits her front door just as a shiny, black limousine enters the street.

She climbs into the limousine and the driver sets off.

*

The traffic is light, but even so, it is 7.55pm when the chauffeur drops her at the end of Downing Street. She exits the limousine, and as she walks towards the police checkpoint, her phone buzzes. "Not another bloody message," she mutters to herself and stops to read the incoming text: "Sara, Bob has just rung. He's told me that if I try to contact you in any way tonight, Suzi and I will be all over the front pages tomorrow. Sorry."

"Shit." She stops and thinks who else she can get to act as her remote bodyguard.

The police officers manning the checkpoint are looking at her impatiently, so she decides to deal with them and ring someone else before she goes in. "Hello," she says, considerably more brightly than she feels. "I'm here to see the prime minister at 8pm. Sara Molan."

"Fine. We've been instructed personally by the prime minister to take your bag, your phone and your coat," says one of the officers.

"Um, I see. I really need the phone. I have to ring someone. I was going to do it when I got inside."

There is no response from the constable.

"I'll just go back around the corner and make the call then."

She walks away from the officers, and once round the corner, she makes a call but only hears this: "You have reached the voicemail of David McDougall. I am sorry I am unable to take your call. Please leave a message after the tone."

"Damn you, David," Sara murmurs to herself as she hangs up without leaving a message. Panicking now, she rapidly scrolls through her directory before selecting another number to dial. She hears a ringing tone and waits.

"Hello," comes the voice on the other end.

"Hello. I need your help."

Soon afterwards, she returns to the police barrier. "Right. Phone, bag and coat," she says as she takes her arms out of the sleeves and then hands all three of the items to one of the officers. In return, they raise the barrier and let her through.

Sara walks slowly to the front door of 11 Downing Street and tells the police officer on duty who she is and why she is there. He opens the door and tells her to go up the stairs to the private quarters on the top floor.

She is still thinking about escaping, but only does so until she remembers the likely consequences. Without her bag and phone, she realises it will be even harder to control the situation she is about to walk into. Once on the top floor, she is surprised by the complete absence of police or security. She wanders along the corridor, looking for a suitable door to knock on. She soon finds one and knocks. There is no response, so she keeps walking forwards and soon finds another door. It opens as soon as she knocks, and Bob Godwin invites her in.

"You look beautiful," he declares, reaching in for a kiss, which Sara manages to partly avoid, and he ends up kissing her cheek.

"Work first," she says with a nervous giggle.

"Quite so. Are you wearing tights or stockings? Do not tell me. Let it be a surprise for later on. Would you like a drink?"

"Not whilst I'm working."

"Well, I'm going to have something to steady my nerves. Interviews terrify me, and you excite me at the best of times. With you dressed like that, I am like putty in your hands."

"That's nice to know," responds Sara with another nervous giggle. "I've had a strange message from William Marshall saying you have told him not to contact me tonight. What makes you think he might?"

"He is your boss. I thought he might want to know how the interview is going. Poor man, he is terrified you are not going to turn up or ruin the interview somehow. I have more faith in you than he does."

"He's terrified all right, but mainly that his wife will find out about Suzi, whoever she is."

"I can assure you, Sara, darling, that it is not his wife he is afraid of."

"Who, then?"

"I would much rather talk about you."

"Well, we can after you've answered my question."

"These days, the police are always interested in anyone cheating on their wife, but one cheating with a little redhead is of particular interest to them – especially when 'little' means young."

Sara gasps. "How young?"

"She is sixteen years old next month. That would be bad enough, but he's been shagging her for three years now."

"No wonder he's terrified."

"Do you want his job?"

"Not yet. I want better, higher-profile presenting jobs first."

"When you are ready, let me know. I can tip off the Metropolitan Police about Suzi, and the job is yours."

"If you are still prime minister."

"Well, that is what the first part of tonight is all about. Anyway, let us talk about you first."

"I thought you knew everything about me. You claim to know about why I left India and… What was it? My sordid affair with Nic. Tell me what you don't know, and I'll be happy to fill you in on the details."

"How good are you in bed?"

"Perhaps you should ask Nic, not me."

"I will find out myself later on. How is Nic, by the way?"

"Nic is fine and living in Marseilles."

"Lucky Nic." Bob pours himself another drink. "Where is your overnight bag?"

"The police took it along with my coat and my phone."

"Excellent. It will be in my bedroom waiting for you later on."

"How do I know you won't report me to the police once we've spent the night together?"

"Well, that would be pretty stupid of me. We would both be in deep trouble. Do not worry your pretty little head about such things. Bob will look after you. Have you ever wondered why you have never been summoned for a virginity test, which you would – of course – fail? Or why young Suzi is the only girl at her school not to be tested annually? As I say, Bob Godwin looks after those who are useful to him. For as long as they do what they are told, of course. Time to tear ourselves away, I think. My media people have set up the cameras in my study next door. They are timed to come on automatically in five minutes. That's just enough time to make ourselves comfortable."

He grabs Sara's arm before she can move away and leads her next door. The study is a small room with a high-quality, large desk in the centre. Two imposing chairs sit side by side behind the desk. Bob guides Sara into the left-hand chair and seats himself in the remaining one.

He confirms, "The cameras are set up on the chairs where they are now – so no fidgeting. The piece of paper in front of you contains the questions. Remember the rules. No changing the questions, no interruptions, no sarcastic comments and no criticism. Understand?"

Sara nods and reads through the questions quickly. In her worst nightmares, she had not expected them to be quite this bad. Once she has read them through twice, she puts the paper where she can see it without glancing down too obviously. They then sit in silence waiting for each camera's red light to come on.

As soon as the two red lights flicker on, Sara starts to speak: "Hello. My name is Sara Molan, and I am broadcasting to you from the prime minister's private study. Alongside me is our current prime minister, Mr Bob Godwin. Welcome, Prime Minister."

"Thank you. I am delighted to have this opportunity to speak to the nation just before the general election campaign starts. It is wonderful to have you, Sara, here to ask the questions."

"Okay. Let's make a start. Prime Minister, would you give us your opinion on the Government's performance in the last five years?"

"I think the party's record speaks for itself. I promised the electorate I would cut crime by 80%. In fact, since I became prime minister, the number of reported crimes has dropped by 83%. So, I have kept my promise and, in fact, have been even more successful than I predicted. This fall in crime is across the board. Murders, rapes, theft, driving offences and all other categories of crime have been cut, cut and cut again. Our streets are safe to walk day and night, and citizens can live their daily lives without fear. In addition, the last five years have seen us winning a war against promiscuity. Anybody having sex outside marriage is committing a crime, and I have personally overseen this drive against the sexual abandon that has plagued this country for decades. The Government has also taken steps to improve the nation's health by offering advice on matters such as vegetarianism and veganism. This has been backed up by limiting citizens' intake of certain items, including chocolate and cigarettes. Good health leads to less pressure on the NHS, less illness, increased production, and a longer and better life for everyone. I want this to be the best country in the world, and we are on the way to that. I have delivered all the promises contained in our manifesto for the 2029 general election. I tell you right now that when I am re-elected prime minister, I will honour every word of the 2034 manifesto. You have my personal guarantee on that."

Sara does not want to put the next question as it is written, but decides not to antagonise the prime minister, and therefore says exactly what is on the paper: "When you win this general election, what can we expect from the next five years?"

"We must not rest on our laurels. Crime is not yet defeated, and I will not stop tackling that problem until there is zero crime. Just think what a wonderful country this will be with all criminals where they belong – in prison, where they can be reformed, or in hell, after a public execution. There are many other areas of life where new rules and regulations are urgently needed. I will introduce compulsory twenty-four/seven opening for all supermarkets, doctors' surgeries, dentists, and all outlets selling food or drink. Corporal punishment will be extended to public organisations such as the armed forces, the police and the NHS. Some powers will be taken away from judges and chief constables. I am very concerned about a recent case where a foreign prostitute was allowed to leave this country without any physical punishment being inflicted on her at all as part of a deal relating to information she had on other criminal activities. There are clearly loopholes in the present Justice Act. They will be closed. No one should be allowed to escape lawful punishment. Finally, as they cost so much money to preserve and protect, I intend to open negotiations with the relevant countries to offload Gibraltar and the Falkland Islands. Oh, I almost forgot – by law, women's skirts will have to reach at least two inches below the knee. Unlike yours, Sara."

Sara smiles at the camera in a somewhat dazed way and reads the next question. "What do you think has been your greatest achievement as prime minister?"

"Definitely driving crime down. Crime is at its lowest rate since records began. I am aware that some ill-informed do-gooders have been critical of some of the methods used. Do not listen to them. My methods work. I will not stop until the country is crime free. In the next few months, I will roll out a number of new criminal offences. I am proud of the progress made on this project, but now we need a final push, which will happen in the next five years."

"What do you think has been the biggest disappointment of your first term as prime minister?"

"From the point of view of the actions of me and my government, I really do not think that there have been any. I have worked day and night to help the country and its citizens recover from the pandemic, a disastrous split with the EU, and the disorder and disunity plaguing this country five years ago. The disappointment is the constant criticism of my hard work by people of lesser ability and intelligence than me. These naysayers are spreading their poison inside and outside Parliament. The media is encouraging them. I will not give these shameful opposers of change the publicity they desire by naming names. They know who I am talking about. The Ministry of Decency, which I set up a few years ago, has not weeded out controversy and unfounded criticism as I had hoped. After this general election, it will be given new powers, which will silence these Moaning Minnies for ever. This will enable me to focus on making this country great, and it will rid the citizens of an unwanted nuisance. I intend to ban pornography of all types, wherever it may be available. I also intend to limit the sale or prescription of contraceptives to married women only. A marriage certificate will have to be produced to purchase these items or to receive a prescription for one, and I am going to ask the Ministry of Decency to check that the couple named on the certificate shown are still married and living together. Penalties for falsely obtaining any form of contraception will include imprisonment and flogging. I mentioned some law and order changes earlier, and I will detail just one more now. The minimum punishment for adultery is to be increased to fifteen years in prison and 2,500 strokes of the nine-tailed whip. Sara, next question, please."

Ms Molan has long since given up on any attempt to pretend she is happy or even that she wants to be in the studio. Wondering when this nightmare will end, she glumly reads Godwin's next written gem. "What about the economy?"

"I'm so glad you asked me that. It took several years to extract the country from the trade agreement with the EU. We now have a marvellous new deal with the USA under President Harris. Unfortunately, it has taken a little longer for the significant gains from this treaty to filter through to us, although this will happen in the next few months. The unanticipated delays have put significant pressure on the country's finances, and it has been necessary to increase taxes by 5% for every taxpayer. I deeply regret this rise, especially as I had genuinely expected to be able to avoid increased taxation. The economy will be stabilised through larger receipts from the USA in the coming months, and I hope that the recent tax rise can be reversed at some point in Common Sense's second term in power. We are finally in an economic position to allow us to move forwards and reap the rewards of being a hard-working, independent country, albeit in an increasingly competitive world. I will continue to oversee investment in and improvement to the nation's infrastructure. We will require additional prisons and punishment centres, and I am hopeful that the long-delayed HS2 project will be able to go ahead in 2037 or 2038. The executive committee of Common Sense has suggested that the project should be renamed in honour of the person who has done so much to ensure that this much-needed transport link does actually reach fulfilment. I am proud to announce that the HS2 project will henceforth be known as the 'Bob Godwin HS2 project.'"

Sara groans inwardly and prepares to ask the final question.

However, the prime minister has other ideas and continues with his remarks on the economic situation: "I would like to ensure the country's economic growth despite the constant uncertainty of the domestic and international currency fluctuations. I have asked the London School of Economics to look at various options, including the revaluation of sterling, currency trades and adopting the US dollar instead of the pound sterling. There are exciting times ahead in the next five years."

Sara jumps in quickly before Bob can start again. "Why should voters give Common Sense a second general election win?"

"Our first five-year term can only be described as a triumph. We have transformed this country into a haven for hard-working, peace-loving citizens. Crime has been virtually eliminated. The economy is recovering slowly, and we have a glorious financial future ahead of us. Today, I have outlined my plans for the next five years. These are for the benefit of every clean-living, law-abiding citizen throughout England, Scotland, Wales and Northern Ireland. Please do not risk this idyll by voting for any other party. Remember, there is only one party run by Bob Godwin. We are common; we talk sense. We are the Common Sense Party. Your vote is valuable; use it wisely and ensure a smooth passage through the turbulence of the next five years. Vote for me. Vote Common Sense. Thank you."

Sara has noticed that the red camera lights are flashing. Whilst having no experience of automatic TV cameras, she guesses that there is little time left. "Thank you, Prime Minister, for everything you have said in this interview. Time has beaten us, so from me – Sara Molan

– and the prime minister – Bob Godwin – goodnight."

Bob turns on her immediately. "I wanted to make a proper goodbye and finish on a real high."

"Look at the cameras. The red lights have gone out. I think I got out with about a second to spare."

"Oh, I see. Time really flies when you are having fun. How do you think it went?"

"You made a lot of points. I hope you haven't confused people by covering so many different subjects. I'm sure everyone is interested in what you plan for the next five years if you are elected."

"When."

"Sorry, I don't understand."

"Not 'if' I am elected; 'when' I am elected."

"You are a long way behind in the polls."

"It was just the same five years ago. Look what happened then."

"You weren't leading the campaign then."

"Exactly. It will be an even bigger margin of victory this time. We are finished here. We will go back next door. There should be some food waiting for us."

Sara follows him back to the room they started the evening in. There certainly is food there: a huge ham joint, various salads, several different fruits, and the *piece de resistance* – a whole salmon lying on a bed of blue-coloured ice. A bottle of champagne in an ice bucket sits alongside the food, and this is the item Bob Godwin heads for.

He opens the bottle and pours the contents into two

champagne flutes. He hands one to Sara and says, "A toast to victory and a great evening's work."

They clink glasses, and Sara – realising suddenly that she needs several strong drinks to ease the numbing of body and soul caused by an hour of listening to the prime minister's general election broadcast – drinks more than half the glass in one go.

"Come on. Tuck in." Bob even manages to make those simple words sound like an order rather than a casual invitation. "I know you will not eat the ham, but do you eat fish?"

"No. I'm vegetarian, not pescatarian."

"Okay. More for me." The prime minster proceeds to carve three slices of ham from the joint before continuing to speak. "You were brilliant tonight. Just what I needed to make me shine."

"I was terrible," Sara replies firmly. "If I wasn't literally trying to save his skin, Marshall would sack me on the spot for an interview like that. No challenging you, no comments, no follow-up questions and not even a change in camera angle. It was almost as dreadful as one of Sue Horton's interviews."

"I am delighted to see that I have not dampened your fire for very long. You are beautiful when you are aroused. Anyway, the plebs will lap it up. You wait and see what next week's polls say. I do not understand how anyone could deliberately avoid superb ham like this. You do not know what you are missing."

"The world is missing a pig. I know that."

"Relax and have some more champagne," suggests Bob, filling her glass.

Sara drinks the whole glass immediately, and before the prime minister can even move away, she offers her glass to him for a refill.

"You never wear a short skirt. You have great legs. In fact, I have no doubt you have a great body. Beauty, brains and ambition. You would make a wonderful wife for, say, a top politician," Bob continues.

Sara looks nervous and empties her latest glass of champagne.

"Let us cut the crap here. Sara Molan, will you marry me?"

"No, of course I won't. You must have drunk more champagne than me. Don't be ridiculous. We don't even know each other properly. I don't love you, and you don't love me. You don't love anybody but yourself."

"I do love you. I have for years. You are all I think about."

"I'm sorry you feel that way. I don't love you. I love somebody else."

"Nic, I suppose. Too busy sunning himself in Marseilles now he has had his sleazy way with you in bed. Your relationship with Nic is just sordid, cheap sex. I am offering you a life of privilege, wealth and eternal love."

Suddenly, Sara is angry and half screams, half shouts her reply: "*You miserable little bastard. You told me you knew everything about Nic and I, but you know nothing.*

SARA

You blackmailed me into coming here tonight. For what? An hour of the world according to high and mighty Prime Minister Godwin, cheap champagne and an even cheaper marriage proposal. I'm leaving now, and I pray that I will never, ever see you again."

Godwin is moving towards her, and as Sara tries to go towards the door, he grabs her and pushes her against the wall. She starts to scream.

"Go on, scream. No one can hear you. I have told everyone here not to come on this floor. The door is locked. It is just you and me." He pushes his body close to Sara's.

She tries to escape by pushing him away, but he is too heavy, and she remains pinned to the wall. She can feel his hands tugging at her skirt and pulling it down to her ankles.

"What a disappointment. You chose the tights. Stupid little slut." Bob raises one hand and slaps her across the face, whilst ripping her tights to pieces with his other hand. Her panties are pulled down next, and Sara can feel his erection against her skin. It is now or never. She summons up what energy she has left and pushes her attacker with every ounce of strength. This time, she manages to catch him slightly off balance, and Bob takes half a step backwards. She uses both hands to push him further away from her and runs for the door, leaving her skirt and pants on the floor in the process. The door is locked, but she bangs on it loudly and yells for help, praying silently that her last minute phone call outside has paid off.

Her hopes are quickly dashed as the prime minister catches up with her and drags her away from the door. He hits her several times until she hits the floor, crying and defeated. Godwin takes off all his clothes and pulls Sara up off the floor. He lets go of her for a second. She takes a step backwards, steadies herself and aims a vicious kick at the prime minister's exposed genitals. Bob doubles up, and Sara heads for the door, once again screaming for help.

She turns back towards the room and sees Godwin coming towards her. He is holding the carving knife in his right hand. Sara shrieks as he pulls her away from the door. She screams as the knife plunges deep into her chest. Sara makes no sound at all as the knife finds another target – her stomach. For her, everything is black by then.

Seconds after the second strike, there is furious banging on the door. "This is Inspector Melville. Prime Minister, open the door."

"Fuck off. You are under orders to stay away from here," commands Bob.

"Break it down," the inspector says to the two officers accompanying him.

A few seconds later, the door frame gives way, and the three policemen find themselves facing a scene they will never forget. The prime minister is standing in the middle of the room, naked and holding a blood-spattered carving knife. Against the near wall, a few feet from the broken door, lies a brown-skinned woman who is naked from the waist down and curled up in a foetal position. She is lying in a pool of blood.

They stand in shocked silence for a few seconds before Melville takes charge. "Maxwell, get an ambulance and get every cop in this place up here pronto. *Now!* Adams, do what you can for her."

The inspector moves slowly towards Bob. "Sir, please give me the knife."

"No. I am going to carve some more ham. It is delicious. Would you like some?"

"Prime Minister, that knife is dirty. You can't use that one. Give it to me, please. I'll get you another one for the meat."

Bob Godwin thinks the police officer's words over and hands the weapon, handle first, to Inspector Melville, who places it temporarily close to him on the dining table.

The inspector then shouts over to Sergeant Adams. "*How is she?*"

"Not good, sir. She's breathing, but it's very weak and ragged. I'm trying to stem the blood, but there's so much of it."

Inspector Melville moves to the other side of the table and grabs a pile of clean tablecloths. Try using these," he suggests as he throws them to Sergeant Adams. "Make a tourniquet. As tight as you can."

Throughout these actions Melville's eyes have never left the prime minister. Now he approaches Bob Godwin. "I think you should sit down. I'll get you some clothes as soon as I can. We'll need yours for forensics." When the prime minister is seated, Inspector Melville talks to him calmly and quietly. "What happened here tonight?"

"We recorded an interview. Then we came in here to eat. She drank champagne, and I ate the marvellous ham. I love her. I asked her to marry me. She said no, but then we started to have sex. I do not remember anything else until I was standing over her, and she was on the floor. Is she all right?"

Inspector Melville looks over at Sergeant Adams. He has managed to tie a tablecloth around each wound. They are no longer white, and the pool of blood on the floor continues to grow, "She's not too good, sir. Sergeant Adams is with her. He's trained in first aid, and there's an ambulance on the way."

"I love her. I just wanted to show her how much I love her. Why are you here? You were told to keep away."

"We received a phone call from a woman saying that someone was in danger in your private quarters. She was insistent that we must investigate."

"Who was it?"

"No idea. She wouldn't give a name, apparently. By the way, who is the lady bleeding on the carpet?"

"Sara Molan. She is a TV presenter."

At this point, Constable Maxwell returns with five other officers.

Inspector Melville says, "Where is that ambulance?"

"Right behind us," Maxwell confirms.

"Great. Are any of you fully trained in first aid?" questions the inspector.

Two hands go up.

"Excellent. Go and help Sergeant Adams until that ambulance arrives." Glancing over to Sara, he sees to his dismay that the sergeant has started cardio-pulmonary resuscitation (CPR) on the patient. "Two of you three, seal this floor off. Nobody comes in or out except paramedics and people who outrank me. Maxwell, find a defibrillator. There must be one here somewhere. Then get some clothes for the prime minister. Be as quick as you can. Frizzell, you stay with the prime minister. Call him 'sir' and get him food if he wants it, but don't let him out of your sight. He is definitely our only witness, and he is also our only suspect at the moment."

The inspector walks out into the corridor just as the paramedics arrive. One enters the room, whilst the other asks Melville, "What precisely have we got?"

"Asian female. Stabbed with a carving knife. My officers have been fighting to keep her breathing," Melville confirms.

The paramedic nods and follows his colleague into the room.

Inspector Melville sighs and dials on his phone. "Hello. I need to speak to the most senior officer on duty. The commissioner or deputy commissioner, preferably."

After a few moments, a voice responds: "I am transferring you to Deputy Commissioner Giles."

A female voice says, "Giles."

"Ma'am, my name is Inspector Melville. Senior duty officer, Downing Street protection squad. I've got a delicate situation here. We went up to the prime minister's private quarters, and as soon as we entered the floor, we could hear a woman screaming. We had to break down the door. Inside, we found Mr Godwin naked and holding a bloody knife. A young Asian woman was lying in a pool of blood on the floor."

"Are you saying the prime minister has stabbed someone in his own rooms?"

"That's how it seems at the moment, ma'am."

"Do the press know?"

"Not to my knowledge, ma'am. I've closed this floor off, allowing nobody in or out but my officers and the paramedics."

"I'm on my way. You take charge until I arrive."

"Yes, ma'am."

Inspector Melville goes back into the room. Prime Minister Godwin is dressed now and eating ham salad. Constable Maxwell comes in with a stretcher. The paramedics put Sara on it immediately, strap her in and head out of the room with all urgency.

Sergeant Adams, who is close to tears, walks over to Melville.

"How is she?" the inspector asks.

The sergeant is unable to answer, but shakes his head sadly.

ACKNOWLEDGEMENTS

I would like to thank Kathy for her remarkable patience, enthusiasm and support during the writing of this book; Ian, Clive and Dilys for their interest in the project; and Sue for listening to me so patiently through the many highs and lows. A big thank you to everyone at Troubador Publishing and Matador for their unfailing professionalism and help. Huge thanks to all my family and friends for their encouragement. Last but not least, thank you to Abby.

For exclusive discounts on Matador titles,
sign up to our occasional newsletter at
troubador.co.uk/bookshop